Seven Times

GW00645257

a

Prisoner

by

Alan P Hadcroft

Co. Author
Hilary A Hadcroft

Knight Writers

59, Jeals Lane, Sandown, Isle of Wight. PO369NS

First published in the United Kingdom in 1995 by Knight Writers

Copyright © 1995 Alan Hadcroft & Hilary Hadcroft

Second edition re-printed in United Kingdom in 2013 by Knight Writers
Copyright © 2013 Alan Hadcroft & Hilary Hadcroft

The following titles by Alan Hadcroft:
DHSS The True Story copyright © 1995
DHSS The Fight Back – *the sun always rises* © copyright

⊣

Printed and bound in the UK by
BEACON PRINT
25 Daish Way, Dodnor Park, Newport, Isle of Wight. PO30 5XJ.
01983 524456

ISBN: 0 9526951 0 3

This book is dedicated

to:

The seven sisters of the Carter family

Best Wishes

Alan Hedenquist

Special thanks to:

all the people who helped in the research of all the facts enabling fact
to be added to fiction, to produce a book of life's happiness and strife.

Also my thanks to:

Mrs Pat Chessell, previously Pat Ovenden

for her toils and patience in proof reading.

Printers

Beacon Print
for printing and binding the book.

Very special thanks to:

Jamie Gerrard

Jamie if you had not made the initial enquiry about the book on facebay, then there would

not have been the interest shown, and we would not have re-printed the book.

We, Alan and Hilary Hadcroft, and the Seven Sisters thank you.

We also thank all the people on Facebay, who have over the years been looking for this book.

Seven Times a Prisoner

It took Alan and Hilary eight months to put this compelling, gripping and sometimes bizarre story together.

It took long days and late nights of mixing fact with fiction to bring you this harrowing tale.

Alan has recently bonded another great relationship with Hilary.
The first being their working one.
The second being their marriage on July 15th 1995.

2013 and Alan and Hilary celebrated their 18th Wedding Anniversary
BUT more importantly
18 years after first being published,
the story of the seven sister's must be told again.

The Facts.

Family Tree.

A. P. Hadcroft.

Seven Times a Prisoner

Prologue

On hearing this strange but true tale about a family named Carter who lived just outside Ryde in the Isle of Wight during the mid to late 1800's, I decided to write a book about it. I changed the names and mixed fact with fiction.

I first heard of the story when I was listening to a phone-in on Isle of Wight Radio. A lady came on-air and mentioned this family and what had happened. I was so captivated by what this lady was saying, that when she'd finished, I rang the station and asked the lady who was just speaking to give me a ring.

Minutes after putting the phone down, two ladies rang me. One was the lady who had been talking about the Carter family, the other lady also knew a lot of history about them. I took in as much information as I could in those few minutes on the phone, and it began to make one of the most fascinating true stories I'd ever heard. The story was great, it was something totally different from what I'd expected for my next novel. This was another true story, a story of suffering, not to one child but to seven!

I didn't bother doing any more research into the actual family, the story was so good that it sparked off my imagination, and the flow of energy that came into my head was entirely out of my control. I just sat there, night after night, this time not having to set out a target of sheets for myself to write. I just wrote until my eyes felt heavy, then I'd look at the clock – which Hilary's brother had made for her – and it would say that it was fast approaching four in the morning.

After three nights of writing, try as I might, I couldn't get back into the story as much as I tried. This was very frustrating for me, as the story by then was really eating away at my brain. I got the urge – I still don't know why – to make up and design the front cover for this story – the first page that anyone buying the book would see. It was impossible to carry on writing, so I bought poster paints, then on an A4 sheet of paper, built up and designed the picture that was in my head.

There it was, the finished cover picture, taped to my reading lamp every night. The picture was of a large house with gardens. There were two large pillars with huge gates on them. I had added seven small girls standing behind the gates ranging in size according to their ages. In the story that was told to me, the children had adopted a stray cat which hung around the gardens of the house. As the years went by, the cat had kittens and the kittens had kittens, until they had in the region of one hundred cats about them. The front cover shows the cat looking in at the children, who were imprisoned behind the gates. I sat there at my desk, just thinking of how to bring such a unique story to paper. Suddenly, with inspiration, I looked at the drawing that I'd done of the house and the children. I looked and looked at it. The children's faces looked more and more real to me, especially three of the hurriedly drawn faces. It was like when you are ill as a child and you are lying in bed, you look up at your patterned curtains, and you can actually see faces in them, and they seem so real it makes you feel uneasy.

I started to jot down all the feelings that I was experiencing from the cover onto my little yellow memo pad, then suddenly, one night while I was sitting there, I started to write. I wrote just pure fiction, making up the whole story all the time, trying to piece together the family and how the house used to be. First Hilary, then my mother, followed by my two children Angie and Adam all noticed a change in my personality. The more fiction I wrote, the more I became the father of these seven children. My family would often remind me that it was only a book that I was writing, but I knew different! It was like these three faces on the drawing I'd done were telling me, no *willing* me to tell their tale and tell it how it really happened.

After all this writing and pressure that I had with the drawing that I'd done, I decided to go in search of the truth, plus adding some fiction to make the story complete, as obviously I wasn't there.

On a Sunday after reaching this decision, Hilary, my mother and I travelled out in our car to find the Carter house and question local people who might have had stories handed down to them from parents or grandparents.

We drove around for more than an hour, travelling from one address to another, hoping that the next one would be the right one. We drove into a yard in East Upton, near Ryde. This was supposed to be the land where the Carter house once stood, but the vibes just weren't there. As soon as I stepped out of the car and onto the slushy mess from where they were now building flats, I knew this wasn't the place. Crouched over, with a chain saw, was a man in his sixties, cutting wood. The smell from the chain saw and burning wood was strange, it penetrated right through my nasal passages.

As I started to talk with the man – it was a little difficult at first, but, as we got further into why I was there, the barrier between my Northern talk to his pure Isle of Wight accent resulted in me finding out that the Carter house – that had long since been demolished – stood three properties away. Directly across the road from the grounds were the old stables, which now housed a gentleman called Miles and his family. It was suggested that I visit Miles as he knew a fair amount about the Carter family.

I drove down to the old stables. As I walked into the cobbled yard I met a young girl. I asked her if a person called Miles lived there. She pointed to a door and then told me that Miles was her farther. I thanked her, then walked with Hilary to the door. After knocking, he appeared and asked us in. He was very helpful. He provided pictures of the family for me and confirmed that directly across from his old stables, once stood the Carter Mansion which had had over thirty rooms. Hilary and I stayed there for nearly an hour, then made an appointment to see him the week after. We left, and walking straight out of the front entrance of the stables, crossed the road to the front entrance of the Carter estate. Miles had been very helpful, but there were still more unanswered questions in my head. I just had to find out more.

Directly in front of us stood two large stone pillars with large balls on top of them. This was crazy – they were the same as I had drawn them on the book cover. Hilary and I agreed that this could be a coincidence. After photographing them we walked through the old gateway and towards a bungalow which had been built on the site.

As we stepped up onto the veranda of the bungalow, we noticed that the large steps that we stood on were covered in beautiful coloured tiles. This was another thing I had written about in my fictional story when describing the entrance hall. Miles later confirmed that the tiles had been the entrance hall floor of the Carter mansion, and carefully saved when the house was demolished. Hilary and I just looked at each other – two things that I had written about.

We knocked on the door several times, but there was no answer. I was itching to investigate the land, as was Hilary. I started walking around to get the feel of the place and how it must have been. I spotted the remnants of the demolition – again as I had written – ruins covered in brambles, rising and falling in stages, an eleven-inch thick wall.... I was beginning to feel uneasy about the whole day. It made me feel as if I'd been willed there by these seven sisters, staring at me through those large, old gates on the cover of my book.

Scrambling over the wall the brambles clawed at my legs. Hilary had difficulty keeping up so I slowed down and helped her. When we reached the flat place I had seen, I photographed the old fireplaces – once full of warmth in that living tomb – the place where those seven little girls had to live from birth to death.

What was happening to me? Was I experiencing all these similarities through their eyes, or – or what? I looked down at the ground and scraped it with my toe – expecting to find just earth, but under about an inch of mossy earth there lay cobbles. Cobbles that must have been from the courtyard. God, I thought. What have I got myself into? This was the last straw, all these things that I'd described before visiting this place, pure coincidence? I couldn't explain it.

As I turned to photograph the whole site, the film ran out in my camera. Nothing strange about that as I knew I was down to the last few shots. We drove straight home after that, but in the car it was so quiet that I knew my mother thought Hilary and I had had words. I was sure that what was happening to me was also happening to Hilary, and we wondered how we could have come so close to the truth, without seeing or talking to anyone.

When we arrived home we were still a little quiet with one another, we all went to our everyday stations. My mother went into the kitchen to make tea, Hilary and I went upstairs to the office. Conversation started to come back in a fashion, I think that the day had really taken us aback. The day had affected us all. I don't think we had expected to find what we did. To me it was mind blowing. I sat down at my desk to go through the paperwork that Miles had given to me. Hilary sat at her desk staring over at me, not really knowing what to say. My mother came in with the tea. The numbness of the afternoon wore off, and we started talking about what we'd experienced. Hilary kept saying that it was *wicked!* My mother and Hilary were talking away as I came to the end of the paperwork. The last document was a clipping about the Carter house being set on fire in 1953. I read it, looked at the Carter girls in the photo, then looked at the top of the clipping. It was from a national newspaper, dated 4th October. My eyes locked on to the date – 4th October that was my birthday! This was the last straw – the one that broke the camel's back. I had to quit this book. It wasn't for me – *no way!*

I walked out of the office, downstairs and into the lounge. Something inside my head told me to stop work on the book, something else told me to carry on. I decided to carry on.

I still had to know more facts about this unusual family, because trying to mix fact with fiction is hard. One can easily contradict the other. Since that Sunday we have done many hours research into this family, finally meeting with the curator of Carisbrooke Castle, who knew the family personally.

This was the inspiration that led to the writing of this novel...

... Seven Times a Prisoner

Edward (Ned) Carter
born 20 September 1848
married 28 August 1884
died 6 May 1931 at East Upton
married
Mary Louisa
born 19 January 1858
died 6 March 1934 at East Upton

Mary Maria
born 9 February 1886 at Puckpool House
died 18 March 1951 – buried 22 March 1951
aged 65 years – unmarried

Edward Hugh
born 1 December 1887
died 1 June 1888
age 7 months

Dorothy
born 24 July 1889 at Puckpool House
died 16 October 1965 – buried 22 October 1965
aged 76 years – unmarried.

Cecily Louisa
born 20 March 1893 at Puckpool House
died 5 May 1977
aged 84 years – unmarried

Gertrude Edith
born 15 December 1894 at Puckpool House
died 29 March 1969
aged 75 years – unmarried

Eve
born 1896
died 26 March 1902
aged 6 years

Aline Barbara
born 4 March 1898 at Puckpool House
died 31 July 1900 at Puckpool House
aged 2 years

Kathleen Martha
born 10 May 1899 at Puckpool House
died 8 September 1948 – buried 15 September 1948
aged 48 years – unmarried

compiled by **R. E. Brinton**

List of Plates

PLATE 1
After asking many people; Hilary my mother and I found the right road in
Ryde, leading to East Upton, where the Carter house used to be.

PLATE 2
This is the lane. There were houses dotted on either side of it as I had written.

PLATE 3

As I stood there with Hilary, staring at the gate posts, it was just as I had imagined it would be. I could picture the gates, the cat, and all the children standing behind them.

PLATE 4
As we walked through the gates the foundations were visible, embraced
by all the brambles.

PLATE 5
The wall of the foundations rose and fell, just as I had written.
This was too much!

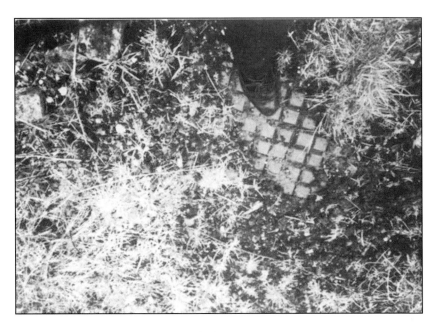

PLATE 6
I scraped my toe on the ground and found the remains of the courtyard.
I felt cold, clammy and tingly.

PLATE 7
As I looked over the bungalow, I saw the large tile arrangement. It was confirmed by Miles that this survived from the great entrance hall.

PLATE 8
The colouring of the tiles is reminiscent of Amari. I had written this as well.

PLATE 9
These old lead urns must have held those carefully chosen flowers, which must have scented the air at those magnificent parties.

PLATE 10
As I turned around heading for the converted stables where Miles lived,
I glimpsed one of the old bedroom fireplaces.
If it had a memory, I wonder what it could tell us, I thought to myself.

PLATE 11
Walking across to the stables, I could picture them as they were, with horses standing in the yard, and carriages strewn around them.

LAST NIGHT'S NEWS

Three lonely sisters of Heartbreak House..

By BARRIE HARDING

FIRE swept through "Heartbreak House" yesterday —and three lonely sisters stood by helpless and watched rooms full of memories destroyed by the flames.

Only three days before, they had shown me round the thirty-roomed mansion at East Upton, high on the hills overlooking Ryde, Isle of Wight, which for years had been their luxuriously furnished home.

In the magnificent house standing on the borders of his rich farmland, Mr. Edward Curter, a former High Sheriff of Hampshire, lived the life of a wealthy country gentleman with his wife and five daughters.

But as the years passed the wealthy squire grew more and more morose, brooding because he had no heir.

When he died, aged eighty-two, in 19—, he left his family leading the life of recluses.

Then one day the daughters found their mother dead. One daughter lingered for years in a nursing home with an in-

Once a luxurious mansion ... now a shuttered ru—

MISS DOROTHY

MISS GERTRUDE

curable complaint. The other four spinsters shut themselves away from the world.

The house died around them. Rich furnishings and expensive carpets rotted. Thieves stripped the roof of its lead.

Then five years ago, Miss Kathleen was found dying of malnutrition beside her a copy of Burke's Landed Gentry.

The three remaining sisters Gertrude, tall, angular and thin with grey straggling hair, Dorothy, short and pale, and Cicely, whom few people have ever seen—moved to a coachman's cottage after treatment in a nursing home.

The property is theirs on trust. But the eventual heir to the crumbling mansion will probably never see it. He is in a French monastery.

Plate 12

After talking to Miles for a while, he gave Hilary and I several photographs and clippings. When I got home that day I looked at the clipping. The date is October 4th 1953. My birthday is October 4th 1944. I knew then that these sisters were asking me, Alan Hadcroft, to tell this tale.

PLATE 13

This is the actual Carter house. It has long been demolished, but the vibes and the foundations still exist. To the seven sisters this was their world. To an outsider it must have appeared to be like Parkhurst - a prison!

PLATE 14
This a copy of a photograph of Edward Carters yacht.
The money they must have had!

FIRE AT EAST UPTON

SOUTH PART OF THE HOUSE GUTTED

Shortly after six o'clock on Saturday morning the Ryde Fire Service were summoned to a fire at East Upton, Havlands, Ryde, which until 1948 was the residence of the Misses Carter, and the south part of the mansion was gutted. Fortunately the firemen were able to seal off the rest of the building, and confine their efforts to subduing the flames, which when they arrived were coming through the roof.

East Upton was for many years the home of the elate Mr Edward Carter J.P., a former High Sheriff of Hampshire and a prominent Ryde resident until his death in 1941. Mrs. Carter died a few years afterwards, and from then until 1948 the Misses Carter had made their home there, living a secluded life. In that year, one of the sisters Miss Kathleen Carter, died, and her three sisters, for reasons of health have since occupied the cottage adjoining the coach-house on the opposite side of the road to the mansion.

When they removed from the house silver and other valuable articles were taken to a local bank for safe custody, but the furniture and fittings including carpets and curtains have been allowed to remain although the house has since been closed with wooden shutters over the windows. The grounds have become badly overgrown on account of there being no staff, and the interior of the house and contents have naturally deteriorated. The mansion has been a temptation for intruders, who in their visits have shown little respect for the contents, and practically all the lead has been stripped from the roof.

The outbreak was first noticed by Miss Cecily and Miss Gertrude Carter who were awakened by the noise of the fire crackling and thought the stables were ablaze. On going to the window, they saw that the mansion was burning, and one of the sisters immediately went to the house further up the road and the fire brigade were summoned by telephone.

Two fire engines, under the direction of Station Officer Cross, were promptly on the scene, and it was found that the fire had apparently started in the lower room at the south-west end of the house which years ago had been used as a schoolroom, and still contained toys and educational equipment. The fire had apparently been burning for some time, as the rooms above were well alight, and immediate measures were taken to save the rest of the house. Firemen scaled ladders to the roof, and fortunately there was an adequate supply of water, but it was several hours before they were able to extinguish the outbreak, and not until the early afternoon were they satisfied that there was no further danger. All the furniture in the damaged portion of the building was destroyed.

The cause of the outbreak remains a mystery, as the house, which contains about 30 rooms, was locked.

PLATE 15
Days after our visit to the Carter house site, we visited the County Press offices in Newport. We found this copy from an edition of the paper printed in 1953

PLATE 16
Later, I was told something about the sisters which related to the first book
I had written. I drove back there to confirm it and found this road, named in
honour of the sisters when the last surviving sister had the well dug.

Contents

CHAPTER 1

On finishing my last book, I had to have several photographs of places in Ryde, Isle of Wight, to complete the story.

As I was walking down this lane, which had several houses dotted on either side of it, I noticed these large cast iron gates to the left of me. The left hand gate was half open, like it wasn't important any more that they should be closed to keep out intruders. Walking across to them and actually clasping my hand around the bars, I had a very funny feeling, a type of sensitive felling of energy, as if the gates and grounds were filled with storage of the past.

Something inside me, urged me to enter, it was like I was being controlled but not out of inquisitiveness. I squeezed past the gate through the small gap and cautiously, step by step, walked about six feet down a path, a path of brambles and tufts of grass. The day was warm and I only had on a short sleeved shirt. There were flies continuously landing on my arms and face, and as I wafted them away, the brambles would claw into my arms. As I groped through the brambles, there was a deep, and I mean deep, smell of fern, the sort of smell that you get on those early evening family walks through the woods. On picking my way through another clump of brambles, which were directly in front of me, I could see the remains of what once must have been a very large house.

I just stood there, motionless, still being pestered by the bugs and flies, but they seemed to become less important to me now, it seemed as if they were putting up their own little protest of my being there. As I gazed at the ruins in front of me, I got this very strong urge to touch them, the whole ground seemed to have an electrifying and childlike dare about it.

Once I'd reached the ruins with my camera clicking away, raising my foot, and then placing it back down on a two stone high wall, I paused. It then started to rise from that point to about six feet then fell back down to a height of about three feet. I climbed onto the highest point of the wall and looked around, it was massive, it must have been a small mansion once of a day. On climbing back down off the wall, I started to explore the ruins and tried very hard to picture and piece the whole house back together. Just to the right of me, looked like it could have been the kitchen, or maybe an outhouse, where the washing might have been done, as it still had the old stone sink there. Just under the overgrown ivy, which looked like it had brought the house to its knees, were dozens of half eaten away with rust, faded labelled, empty tins of cat food. At the time didn't mean a thing to me, as anybody could have dumped them there, but I did think that this was the sort of thing that caused health hazards! Scrambling across another piece of stone, with sharp brambles out of it, I came to another free piece of land.

As I glanced to the left, this time there was a pile of chard wood, and seeing the spindles, I assumed that, that was the remains of the staircase. Across from that was a large piece of land with just a few clumps of stones lying there. I quickly headed for that place. It was like I wanted to see the whole place at once. As I walked onto this pretty level piece of ground, my feet seemed to sink into it. With the toe of my shoe, I scratched the earth and ash away, and to my surprise, there were large blue and white enamel tiles. Yes! I was right, this had been a large house at one time, and this must have been the reception hall. Standing there, I felt happy, as if I could burst into song, and yet, at the same time, I felt sad. It gave me a very uneasy feeling.

A bird flying over me gave a coo, to which I lifted my head gazed up at the sky, then slowly dropping my head and eyes, I scanned the trees and bushes all around me. Turning full circle, I gave out one hell of a shriek, as there standing directly behind me, was a very old man. He was not dressed very favourably, in fact, he looked like a tramp. He was thinning on top of his head, with uncombed hair hanging over his ears. He wore a dirty cream shirt, with an old grey cardigan with holes in the elbows. His trouser bottoms were tucked in his socks, and the shoes he wore were dropping off his feet.

"God," I said. "You nearly gave me a heart attack."

"Sorry nipper," he said. "I always comes 'ere of an afternoon for me walk."

I told him that I'd just stumbled on the place by chance, and I was inquisitive to what it was, and what had happened to it, for it to get into this state.

We started to walk around together, looking at different places, it was like he was giving me a guided tour. He explained what room was what, and in fact, he gave me a pretty detailed view of what the house looked like. We walked from the ruins towards a wooden bench, which he'd obviously cleared free of brambles over the years with his everyday visits, for a sit down. As we sat there, the sun beating down on us, I could see him through the corner of my eye, just staring at the ruins, as if a part of him belonged there. I asked him what sort of people had lived there, were they royalty?

"No nipper," he said. "When I've told you this tale, you'll never forget it."

I smiled and rested back on the bench, beads of sweat forming on my brow, waiting for him to begin. After listening to him for about an hour and a half, I just couldn't believe it, and yet, I could, as I'd sensed something very strong as he was telling me the tale.

This strange tale, was one of the strangest, I have ever heard in my life. Normally, you'd just listen to it, and think that the person who was telling you, had just walked out of the 'tall story club'. If it weren't for the fact that this family really existed, you'd fast forget it.

CHAPTER 2

For days and days after, the tale just kept running through my head. I could imagine the life style of this family, and I could picture the old stone house, well it was a type of mansion.

The life style that they led, was very grand. The estate had been handed down through the generations, and the last member of the Browning family to live there was William.

William Browning was a highly respected barrister, who socialised with the gentry of the day. Browning was a well-known figure with the locals. He would hold regular parties at his mansion, and the locals would often see people of status rolling up in their horse driven carriages. The men would be dressed in top hat and tails, while the ladies would be wearing the latest fashioned silk ball gowns, with large bustles at the rear.

There were plenty of butlers and maids on duty, whenever there was a party. The gardens leading up to the house, would have oil lamps and candles strategically placed, giving off a gossamer effect on the trees and shrubs, making the gardens a magical, romantic escape. To the locals, it looked like something out of a Cinderella ball.

All around the grounds, there would be the sweet smell of carefully chosen night flowers. The air around the house would be filled with the sound of the orchestra, and ladies gaily laughing behind their ostrich feathered fans.

The parties would go on until the early hours of the morning. Business deals would be made, wives would make excuses, and then slip, un-noticed into the gardens, to meet their lovers.

It was at one such party, that William met Amelia, the woman who was later to become his wife. While all the other young women were flitting and flirting from one eligible suitor to the next, Amelia would be deep in conversation with the more mature guests. It was clear to William, that she had had a very sheltered upbringing. She was innocent to the ways of life, and this was a great attraction to him.

William lived alone in his huge stone mansion, with just the companionship of his servants and trusted butler. The large ivy clad stone steps leading up to the front door, brought you into the impressive hallway. The Amari tiled floors, an imported gift from China, led to the completely spindled staircase. The walls on either side of the stairs, were covered with grand pictures of Williams ancestors. Plants were carefully placed to complement the furniture, while vases full of beautiful smelling flowers stood on any flat surface.

Just to the right, at the foot of the stairs, were two large oak doors, which swung open into the ballroom, which was really something! It had polished wood floors, seating all around, a small stage at the far end for the orchestra, and just to the side of the stage, were the massive French windows, which led out onto the balcony overlooking the gardens. On the night of the balls, these windows would be left open, so that the guests could cool down from the dancing by strolling round the gardens.

Across from the ballroom, was the study, again with large oak doors. All the walls but one were panelled. The un-panelled wall was completely covered with books. By the grand stone fireplace, there were two big, leather winged chairs facing each other. This, according to William, was the best room in the house.

The rest of the ground floor consisted of another twenty rooms, plus the kitchen and morning room, and off the upstairs landing were eight bedrooms, and four bathrooms.

It was a well-known fact, that the Tzar of Russia was a regular visitor at the Browning parties, it was also common knowledge with the staff, that for all their fineries, they would often use their beds as toilets, but they wouldn't dare tell their master, as a good position was hard to come by.

William would rise early in the morning, to find his clothes neatly laid out for him. He would be helped to dress, then he would make his way down the stairs, briefly looking at the portraits on the wall, passed the plants and flowers in the hallway, to the dining room for his breakfast. He found it hard to concentrate on things, as his mind was taken up with thoughts of Amelia, dear, sweet, beautiful Amelia. The young woman he'd fallen so deeply in love with, that night at the ball.

Many a day past, then came the night of his next party. The usual guests had arrived, the flirtatious young women looking for husbands, the matchmaking mothers trying to find partners for their elder daughters, the young men, with an eye for a good time with a pretty face, and there, at the back of the room Amelia.

She was dressed so elegantly, so beautifully, so femininly. Her face shone with her beauty, a face un-blemished by the latest mask of cosmetics, that was so popular at the time.

He watched as she glided around the ballroom on the arm of suitor after suitor, he watched, as young man after young man went to talk to her, knowing that one of these handsome young men, could ruin his whole life.

He found it hard to make small, polite talk to his guests, so, at the stroke of midnight, he decided to make his move. If she accepted his advance, he knew that would be the turning point in his life, the start to future happiness.

He walked across to Amelia, who was standing talking to an elderly Army Major. As he neared the group, he found himself drain, he didn't know what he would say to her, if in fact, he could speak at all.
She turned to face him with a smile, a smile he would never forget. From that moment on, he knew he really did love her. He had a strange feeling in the pit of his stomach.

"Good evening William." She said. The minute she spoke to him, the nervous feeling disappeared, and he felt completely at ease with her. He simply asked if he could speak to her on the balcony, away from the hullabaloo of the ball room.

"Of course, but could you just give me a few minutes." She replied.

He turned away, with a slight nod of the head, not believing she'd follow him, but still he carried on, through the dancing guests, vaguely hearing people calling his name, but unable to answer. As he reached the balcony he closed the doors behind him, sipping hurriedly from his glass of champagne, wondering what reason he could give if she did not follow. Lost in his thoughts, listening to the orchestra playing, he knew that he was tired of this life style. He wanted only to be with Amelia.

He watched other couples walking in the gardens, and flirtatious young men and women playing hide and seek between the bushes and round the trees. He smiled with nervous anticipation.

The music suddenly became louder, and William realised that the French windows had opened. Holding his breath, he slowly turned round, and there in the doorway, light shinning behind her, stood Amelia. It was like a light from heaven had shone down and was surrounding her.

As they stood, looking deeply into each other's eyes, both knew that they were instantly and deeply in love.

Over the next few months, the parties became few and far between. The locals would often see William and Amelia walking hand in hand through the gardens on those warm summer evenings. It was clear to each other that they were in love.

William decided it was time, and on one such walk, he asked Amelia to become his wife.

CHAPTER 3

It was soon the morning of the wedding, the whole house had been cleaned from top to bottom. The caterers had delivered the food for the wedding breakfast. The hall was laden with vases of beautiful smelling flowers. William had hired extra staff for the occasion, they had been inspected and inspected, extra starch was put in the aprons to crisp them up, caps whitened, and hair pinned securely under them.

In the ballroom the guests were standing waiting, sipping champagne, and waiting for the local priest.

William walked down stairs, for the final inspection of his staff. He went down the line off young men and girls holding their hands out in front of them, first palms up, and then turning them over. At the end of the line, William's butler, in a stern voice said: "Right girls and boys, quickly and with grace, go to your stations."

With excitement, the line dispersed, some went to the kitchen, some to the dining room, some up the stairs, and others into the ball room and the waiting guests

The atmosphere grew more intense, as the time drew nearer the beginning of the ceremony. Most of the guests were taking their seats and talking quietly mumbling to themselves, but with one ear open and waiting for the formalities to began.

The priest had arrived, and was stationed by the organist, waiting to give word of the bride's arrival. Suddenly a small boy, one of Amelia's nephews, came running down the aisle towards the priest. As he reached the priest, William was making his own descent down the rows of people towards the makeshift alter. As he walked down, he could see the small boy talking to the priest, then as quickly as he had run down, he started to run back, getting closer to William, the small boy seemed to slow down as he neared William, who hesitantly looked at him smiling, the boy smiled back, and ran off. A quick flash ran through his mind of how his and Amelia's son would look in years to come.

The old man beside me then stopped his story. He pulled out a large white handkerchief to wipe his brow free of the sweat from the warm day. I didn't think of it at the time, but later that day, I was suprised that he had such a fine white handkerchief, compared to the way he was dressed.

I stood up and stretched my legs, I brushed my head with my right forearm. I walked about six feet from the bench, and looked across towards that large open space, that had once been the ballroom. I could picture them all there, it made me feel exceptionally happy.

Suddenly I heard: "Nipper! Nipper! There's more, and it gets worse." As I walked back towards where he was sitting on the bench, I couldn't help glancing over my shoulder, back to the spot that was once the ballroom.

Fascinated I sat back down, this tale wasn't like any I'd heard before. I drifted back to the wedding, it felt like I was actually there, everything seemed so real........

As William approached the priest at the make shift altar, the priest bent down and asked if he was ready. William nodded his head, a life long friend got up and stood on his right hand side. William glanced to his friend and nervously smiled at him, "Yes William, I've got the ring, and I couldn't be happier for you." he whispered.

"I'm glad someone is." William said dryly. Since his engagement had been announced, he had lost a lot of so called friends, the type of friends who were only interested in his parties. Silently they both looked at the flower arrangements on either side of the alter.

William could hear a few guests coughing, and quietly whispering behind him, then the murmuring became over-powered by the sound of the organ, playing the traditional wedding march.

Williams heart beat quickened, as Amelia started to walk down the make shift aisle towards him. William could feel the beating in his temples, and thought that at any time his head would explode.

He could feel Amelia getting closer to him, and suddenly, she was there, standing at his side. He turned his head to look at her, his beautiful Amelia, looking so innocent, compared to the women he had once known, she was an angel of purity.

The priest started to read the Marriage Service, Amelia insecurely searched with her hand for Williams, then finally she found his little finger, and entwined hers with his.

Then, after the final 'I will' they were pronounced man and wife. That was it, they were bonded in life, to love and cherish each other. William turned to Amelia, put his hands lovingly around her waist and drew her near. Tenderly, he kissed her, to the delight of the gathered congregation, who clapped their hands enthusiastically, half because they did not think William would ever settle down, and the others because they were happy for them both.

While the priest congratulated them, and the other guests gathered into small groups around the ballroom, the servants quickly cleared away all the chairs that had been used during the ceremony.

William and Amelia turned around to face the guests who had gathered in small groups around the dance floor. They raised their glasses, which by then had been refilled with champagne, and toasted the happy couple.

The buffet was quickly set up, the orchestra assembled, then, the party of all parties began.

There was laughing, joking, dancing, and when the odd person had had too much to drink, they were without fuss, shown through the door. The party carried on through the night and into the early hours of the morning, until most of the guests had either retired to their rooms, or gone home.

William and Amelia walked through the open French doors and onto the balcony, where their eyes had first united.

William had his jacket off, his bow tie was undone, yet Amelia still looked as fresh as she did when she first walked down the aisle to him. They walked hand in hand through the gardens, but this time it was different, they were man and wife.

The early morning risers who lived around them, could see them wondering arm in arm, they knew from then on, there would be no more late night parties at the Browning house to keep them awake. No more clattering of horse shoes, no more squeaking carriage wheels clattering down the road. Those days were over, and it was bliss!

11

William and Amelia, in the warmth of the early morning haze, strolled back to the house. The servants had been working all night, and had nearly cleaned away the aftermath and debris from the wedding.

They walked up the stairs, past the flowers that again were giving off their exquisite fragrances. They walked towards Williams' rooms. Behind the closed door, they kissed and held each other closely. They were happy at that moment just being alone together, and able to hold each other.

They dropped down onto the bed, face to face, and still holding each other, just pecking each other lightly on the check and lips, until they both fell into a deep and happy sleep.

The next thing they knew, it was coming light again, they'd slept through the whole of the day and night, and awoke the following morning.

CHAPTER 4

Things were great between them, time had no meaning, they had each other, they were in love! Love neither had ever experienced before.

That morning they made love for the first time, it was beautiful, a coming together of two people as one.

Amelia left William in bed, while she decided to get the feel of the house that he had lived in all those years. She had only ever seen it as a party guest, where the only rooms to be seen, were the ballroom, and downstairs cloakroom. She was now to see it as the 'lady' of the house.

It took her only a few minutes to dress in something comfortable, yet presentable, as the servants would have been up since six preparing breakfast. She tiptoed across the bedroom, so as not to disturb William, who was sleeping soundly through contentment of being with the woman he loved. As she pulled the bedroom door gently shut, she found herself on the grand landing. She could see all the way down the long hall to the top of the stairs.

Beams of bright sun light shone through the windows, and settled gently on the patterned carpet before her. Taking a few steps, her left arm rose and delicately stroked the face of a grand marble bust that stood on a pedestal against the wall. She was blissfully happy, she was deeply in love. William was the only man for her. With increasing confidence She started to spin around and around gracefully, humming a tune as she moved nearer to the top of the stairs. She gently cupped the petals of flowers, still on display from the day before, smelling their delicate perfume.

As she reached the top of the stairs, she was happy, she felt like a child again. Looking quickly around to make sure none of the servants were around, she climbed onto the banister, and slid all the way down to the bottom of the staircase, giggling happily to herself. This is what she'd always dreamed of. A nice home, a man she really loved, and children. She must be the envy of every woman alive, she thought to herself.

As she got off the banister, she straightened her skirt, she walked across the hall, gazing at all the paintings hanging on the walls. She walked past the centre hall table, dragging her middle finger on it. Yes, this really was happening to her.

She walked across to the morning room were the breakfast was served, taking in all the smells that where coming from the kitchen. It was a mixture of bacon, kidney and toast, but the smell that over powered all of them was the fresh ground coffee.

As she entered the room, she walked across to the fire place, and pulled a long cord suspended from the ceiling. She found her seat at the grand oak table, and waited for the maid to arrive.

After she'd eaten just enough to satisfy her appetite - because to her, maintaining her figure, was of the utmost importance - she walked back to the ballroom. She swung open the doors, and just stood there, gazing around remembering what had taken place there two days ago. As she stood there, smiling to herself, two hands were placed on her shoulders. For a split second it made her jump, and as she turned her head, she saw it was William. His head leaned closer to her, then he kissed her neck, "come on," he whispered. "Come back to bed. We are man and wife now, we are supposed to have a family." They smiled at each other. It seemed to her, that he couldn't wait to be a father. She wasn't going to argue, as she longed for a child too. A child that was from him to her, the ultimate token of their love!

Twelve weeks later Amelia knew, after all the sickness, irritability, and generally feeling poorly, she was pregnant!

CHAPTER 5

William was out in Ryde town somewhere on business. Amelia couldn't wait for him to arrive home. She had to tell him, even though it hadn't been confirmed by the doctor yet that she was pregnant.

It was one of the longest days in Amelia's life, waiting for William to return. She sat on the big stone steps, that lead to the house, elbows on her knees, her chin cupped in her hands, waiting for him to walk through the huge iron gates at the bottom of the garden.

Suddenly the gates creaked open. Amelia raised her head, she was still waiting on the stone steps, it was William. Immediately she stood up, ran down the steps and across the lawn, brushing past shrubs and bushes, straight into the arms of her beloved William.

"How has your day been darling?" she said.

"Fine my love." He replied.

She thought that she would wait until dinner before telling him the good news. As they walked back through the garden to the house, she had her arm around him, and nestled her head on his left shoulder. She felt good. She felt clever at conceiving his child, she couldn't stop smiling.

This was a big thing for Amelia, it meant even more happiness and security for her. She wasn't like all the other women having babies, this one was theirs, this baby was special.

During their evening meal, she toyed with whether or not to tell William, after all, it hadn't been confirmed yet, but yet she **knew**, she knew she was. As she sat there eating, she kept smiling to herself and hoping that William would catch on to her secret, but he never said a word, he just kept eating his dinner.

Later, after they had retired to the bedroom, after some small talk on the days activities, William fell asleep, tired after his days toils. But Amelia just lay there, eyes wide open thinking of how and when to tell William.

In the early hours of the morning, while William was sleeping peacefully beside her, she decided that later that day, she would travel into the town of Ryde. She would visit the family doctor, so that he could confirm her pregnancy.

The Browning family doctor, was also a close personal friend of Amelia's. He had known her since she was a little girl, and looked on her as one of his own daughters. He asked the usual questions, did the usual tests, and told her that within the next couple of days he would call round with the answer.

The next two days were tremendously anxious for Amelia. She wanted to tell William that she thought she was expecting his child, but she couldn't , just in case she was wrong.

It was nearing lunchtime, when the rusty old gates creaked open. Just to the left of the house, Amelia was in the garden pruning the rose bushes. As she heard the gates opening, she looked up in their direction. There stood the doctor, with his tiny black bag in his hands. He still had that stern look on his face, the look of authority. I suppose it must be part of their job, not to give any secrets away be they good or bad, she thought to herself.

She immediately stopped pruning the roses, and dropped the scissors. Her heart sank, she had done what many other women had done, and judging by the look on his face, she was wrong, she wasn't pregnant. As she walked across the lawn to the doctor, she saw him wiping his brow with his handkerchief, she still got the same emotions from him. He was still stern faced, but his face also said that he was glad to see her. The secret he held was locked in him until they were two feet apart.

"Amelia," he said. "Congratulations, you are pregnant."

She immediately felt herself light up within, and a huge smile formed on her face. "Thank you doctor, thank you." She said leaning forward and kissing him lightly on his check.

"Now you hear me Amelia, you take it easy from now on."

"I will, I will." She said softly. "Trust me doctor, I'll do as you say."

She offered him a fresh glass of lemonade, seeing as it was such a hot day, but he declined, saying that he had a few other people to see that afternoon.

As he walked away, he kept glancing back at Amelia, and she could see in his eyes, that he'd meant what he'd said about resting. She also knew that this would not be, by any means the last time she'd see him.

As the gate creaked open, and the doctor was on his way to visit his other patients, Amelia turned towards the house and couldn't believe it. Inside her, there was a life growing, her child, their child. My goodness we are clever, we have done it, we are soon to be a proper family she thought.

As she reached the stone steps which led to the front door, she turned around again, and sat down. She was in a world of her own. She must have been sat there for about ten minutes, then something startled her out of her day dream.

The heavy iron gates had creaked open again, and there stood William, jacket off and held with one finger over his shoulder. His waist coat was open wide, his tie dropped. That day it was hot, and what ever business he had been on, must have exhausted him.

She stood up, and ran towards him, yearning to tell him the good news. But she realised that a good bath, a rest and some dinner would give him time to relax, then would be the perfect time to tell him the news.

Later that evening, while they were sat in the morning room, she decided to make his day complete.

"William." She said.

"Yes my dear."

"There's something that you should know."

"Yes Amelia, please tell me quickly, as I'm very tired."

"I'm going to have our child."

Even though his eyes were half closed, they sprung to life. "What are you telling me?"

"I'm pregnant."

"That's marvellous," he said, sitting up in the arm chair that he'd slouched back in.

From that moment on, there wasn't a thing Amelia could do, without William watching her carefully. He was a changed man, a man preparing for the arrival of his child. A man who would live totally for his family.

As the months progressed, William cushioned Amelia's every move to protect her and their unborn child. His days of going off to Ryde Town, had ended. He was quite content strolling around the house or the gardens, with Amelia at his sides, their arms linked.

The few servants that were left at the Browning house, would tell the residents around the estate of how William would do almost anything for Amelia. He was obsessed with Amelia having his baby.

The months soon passed from that hot July, and before William and Amelia realised it was March. Amelia was two weeks past her time, and William was worried out of his mind. He was afraid that she would lose the child, even though the doctor was visiting regularly.

One evening, while William was giving the babies room a final going over, making sure that the nursery was equipped with everything a new born baby would possibly need, and Amelia was in the living room downstairs, he suddenly heard her cry out for help. For the past three weeks, he had engaged the services of a midwife to live in the house with them, should Amelia need her at a minutes notice.

William ran out of the nursery and down the long corridor. His heart was pounding, his only thought was to reach Amelia as quickly as he could, all the way down the corridor and as he descended the stairs, he was shouting for the midwife.

"Damn you, damn you!" He shouted. "Where are you?"

As he rushed through the living room doors, to his surprise the midwife was already standing at the side of Amelia, who was seated on one of the hard back chairs.

"There's no need to panic Mr. Browning." The midwife told him. "It's the most natural thing in the world."

She then left Amelia, and headed for the kitchen, passing William she gave him a very stern look of I know what I'm doing. William gazed after her in amazement, noticing just how calmly she was taking it all. He seemed to relax a little then, knowing that she was only a few rooms away, and obviously had the situation under control.

Amelia started to pant again and gripped the back of the chair next to her. William noticed that the knuckles of her hand were pure white, and that her arm was shaking. He glanced back at her face, she wasn't making a sound, but he could see the pain. She fixed her eyes on him, and he knew that he couldn't do a thing for her. He was helpless, he could only stand there, and watch Amelia, who for the first time in her life was going through such pain, pain that a man could never imagine.

The midwife walked back into the room and went straight to Amelia, William looked at her, and quickly flashed his eyes back to Amelia, who had started to pant again, but this time even harder. Hurry he thought to himself, please hurry and help her.

"It's time now." The midwife said gently to Amelia. "Lets try and get you to the bedroom shall we."

William rushed across to her side and took her by the right arm.

"At her own time Mr. Browning, if you please."

Just then, there was a loud knocking at the front door. William was unsure of what to do. He wanted to stay and help Amelia, yet the servants weren't answering the door.

"Will you be all right darling?" he asked, "just while I see to that racket."

"Yes, of course." Amelia replied.

He rushed out into the hall just before one of the servants arrived.

"Where the hell have you been?"

"Sorry Sir," she replied. "I was bringing logs in for the fire."

"Attend the door, and be quick." he ordered.

"Yes Sir." She replied giving him a small curtsy.

By this time, Amelia had entered the hall, and on passing William she paused for a few seconds. "William, it wasn't her fault." she gently said. Then carried on walking with the help of the midwife, across to the stairs.

The maid opened the door, with the grace she'd been taught from her mother when she was a small child. She had been taught to open the door slowly, it always gave the caller the feeling of inferiority.

As she pulled open the door, there stood the doctor. He looked at William, with a look that took William aback. He knew that this was the man who was going to make Amelia all right, make his family complete. William welcomed him with open arms.

As both men hurried up the stairs towards Amelia's room, the doctor knew that the midwife would be in complete control, as she would have more experience in childbirth than he would ever have in all his years in his practise.

As they rushed along the landing, the moon beams shinning through the windows, the moans from Amelia were growing stronger and stronger. As William and the doctor reached the bedroom door, William paused for a while. It was as if he knew that he was going to be disappointed. He had his heart set on a boy.

He walked into the room, and went over to join the doctor.

"Give me room, give me room." The doctor ordered.

William moved to one side, and watched in amazement, as the doctor and midwife did their job, one talking to the other. It looked easy, he thought, almost as easy as saddling a horse.

Suddenly, there was the cry of a new born baby, both the doctor and midwife looked over to him and smiled. The midwife lifted into her arms, the small reddish, crinkled baby, another life, a little person who was totally dependent on them, and them alone.

The doctor tore up a piece of sheeting for the midwife to wrap the new born in. William was so very happy. The midwife turned to him and said, "Congratulations Mr. Browning, it's a girl, and a beautiful one at that."

Amelia and William looked at each other, they both smiled. She held out her arms to embrace him, and he fell gently, so as not to hurt her, into them.

CHAPTER 6

The morning after, William opened his eyes to the sunlight shining through onto the wall of the bedroom. As he looked around, he suddenly realised that Amelia wasn't beside him. She like a hawk, had risen and after relieving the midwife of the newly born child, had made her way down to the dining room to have her breakfast.

William couldn't rest without Amelia next to him. He tried, even with the headache that he had, to fall back to sleep, but he kept waking, time after time, until he rose and dressed. As he rushed down the landing towards the stairs, he constantly called her name. On the bottom step of the stairs, still calling for Amelia, he heard her voice softly coming from the dining room.

As he entered, he saw Amelia sitting at the large table eating a bowl of porridge, and to the right of her, laying on a small blanket, well covered, was their tiny bundle of joy. Amelia glanced up for a second from watching the baby, and wished William good morning. He looked at them both and smiled, a smile with a difference, a smile of inner happiness. He walked across to them, first leaning over and giving Amelia a gentle kiss on the top of her head, then bending down further and kissing the little baby girl, while stroking her face with his little finger. Just then, one of the older female servants walked into the kitchen.

"Would ma lady like me to take the child and dress her?"

"Yes, please," Amelia said, " but *please* be careful."

The old lady smiled, and walked across to the baby, she picked her up with both arms and whispered gently to the child as she walked out the room. William sat down at the side of Amelia, who was glad, as she had something on her mind, and that was the baby's name. She'd got it fixed in her head to name the child after her favourite aunt, but she wanted it to appear that the name came for William's choosing, and not hers.

Firstly she gave him three names that she really liked, and like all men he choose the wrong one. Amelia had to then start to find all the faults and flaws with the two names that she really didn't want. Eventually, William came up with a name for the child – the one that

Amelia had set her heart on – simple really. The baby was now known to the world as Clementine.

As time went on, little Clementine grew into a healthy, bouncy one year old. There was nobody like this little girl to her papa. He would arrive home during the day from some business in Ryde, to play with her for hours and hours in the gardens of their home. William would do this regularly with Clementine, and it wasn't long before she was walking. William would sometimes just sit and watch her, looking at her every feature. It was like he was watching a complete replica of his wife, with her dark hair and beautiful big brown eyes, how he loved them both.

One day Amelia came out of the house as usual with Clementine to let her play in the sunshine, knowing very well that William would be home within the next fifteen minutes. As Clementine was bending over and plucking all the heads off the daisies, Amelia sat down on the large stone steps that led to the house. Soon William was home, flinging his jacket onto the grass, he was soon rolling over and over with Clementine on the grass, finding more daisies to pluck. With her knees raised, and head cradled in her hands, Amelia just watched them, it made her feel good watching her husband dote over his little girl. After a while, he spotted Amelia sat there smiling. He laid Clementine down on the grass nearby, and walked up to the top step where Amelia was sitting, and sat down beside her. As they watched Clementine playing, they started to talk about how nice it would be if Clementine had a brother to play with, a brother to look after them both while they were growing up. Amelia turned to William and said how lovely Clementine was, he smiled and nodded his head. He knew how it would be if they had a boy! A boy who could do all the things with his father, while Clementine could learn her role from her mother, what a perfect family they would be. With his arm around her shoulder, he gently pulled her towards him and kissed her on the forehead. She looked up at him, and gently kissed him on the lips. William rose and quickly ran down the steps, scooping Clementine up in his strong arms. As he walked back to Amelia, he told her that he thought they should now retire for the evening meal, and take an early night. She looked at him, her face had a kind of glow about it, but her eyes told all to William, they had that watery glassy look about them, a look of a person with such warmth and passion in them. It told William that she was ready, ready for the ultimate surrender, a surrender to the one she loved, and most importantly of all, to try for another baby.

After they had their evening meal, and Clementine had been laid down for the night by the nanny, William and Amelia sat back in the large winged chairs in front of a large log fire in the study that William loved so much. The clock struck ten, William glanced across to Amelia, then smiled; she knew the moment he'd smiled that it was time to go to bed, so she stood up and slowly disappeared out of the room, and in the direction of the bedroom........

The morning after, William was up, washed, dressed and away on business, long before Amelia started to wake. She woke gradually, with thoughts of the night before still in her head. She thought of the things that had been said and the affection shown towards her. She had an overwhelming feeling that she had once again pleased William and was pregnant.

The day soon passed, and so did the months. Amelia, after getting confirmation from the family doctor, was indeed pregnant again, and after telling William the good news, they both were looking forward to the new arrival. Clementine, by this time was well over one year old, and she too, in her childish way, was anxiously awaiting the new brother or sister that was on the way.

William was like a two year old, he was over the moon! First of all he'd married the most beautiful girl on the Island, secondly, she'd given him the most exquisite little girl imaginable, and now, to make his dreams complete, this time she was sure to have a son. A son who he could share all the joys of boyhood with, like his father did with him. They could explore the gardens together, climb trees, and best of all, they could spend many hours together just enjoying the piece and tranquillity that fishing would bring them.

As soon as the news got around that there was to be another addition to the family, people that they knew and close friends started to call on them. Most of the callers probably wanted to know the latest gossip first hand, the rest out of genuine concern for the Brownings. Little Clementines feet did not touch the ground over the next three months, with being passed from one set of arms to the next. But, as it always does, the novelty soon wore off with the Brownings 'friends'. They'd scrutinised the family's life style, compared it to theirs, and how William used to live, and their curiosity had been satisfied. As soon as they had all started to visit, they stopped.

The nine months soon passed, and Amelia was on a day to day count down. The midwife had again been moved into the Browning household and was on standby ready for the big moment. One night William was in his study, with the large log fire crackling before him, he lay back in one of the large winged back chairs, with his feet resting on a tuffet, he lounged there just staring at the flames dancing in front of him, with a large brandy in his hand. Amelia had retired some hours earlier, with slight twinging pains in her stomach. He closed his eyes for a moment – half through tiredness and half through the effects of the brandy. Suddenly he heard a cry of "master! *MASTER!* Come quickly it's time." He opened his eyes wearily, unsure if he had been dreaming or not. He listened out for more cries, but heard none. With him sitting directly in front of the fire, he was sweating, his neck and gullet were dripping wet. He felt weak and drained, like a force was being drawn out of him, a force that Amelia must have been experiencing, he lay there panting and listening to the logs crackle in the grate, then the shouts started again,but loader this time.

"Sir, *SIR,* come quickly!"

He put all the strength he could gather into standing up and walking towards the study door which he opened as wide as he could. The cold air of the hall hit him immediately. Yes he thought, this is it. Rushing past the open mouthed maid, he sped two steps at a time up the staircase and towards the room that Amelia was in.

As he entered the room, he saw Amelia propped up in the bed with four large pillows covered with silk pillow cases, cushioning her back and sides. She was well lit with the large oil lamp that was on the chamber cupboard at the side of the bed, giving William a perfect illusion of mother and child. Amelia lay there with a tiny bundle in her arms, she was dripping with sweat after her ordeal, the midwife was slumped in the bedroom chair near the fire, she looked drained.

As William stood at the bottom of the bed staring at Amelia and their child, the midwife rose from her seat, and without saying a word, simply walked out of the room with a look on her face of 'I've done it again.' William smiled, Amelia looking up from the child said " William, please take her and give her to the nanny, I'm *so* tired." She lay back on the pillows that had comforted her all night, and closed her eyes, with a movement of it's all over now, I'm back to normal, then dropped into a well overdue sleep.

William gently lifted the new born child out of the arms of Amelia, and turned down the oil lamp. This was the end to a very important day. He carefully carried the child across the room towards the door where the nanny, although exhausted, was waiting. As she took the child with such carefulness from William, he couldn't help but think what a wonderful woman she was. Still feeling drained, William watched as the nanny carried the baby gently to the nursery where Clementine was, after he had closed the door, nodding goodnight, he retired to one of the guest rooms, in order not to disturb Amelia.

CHAPTER 7

The morning after, just like when Clementine had been born, Amelia was up and joining William at the breakfast table. This morning was the same as all the other mornings that he'd been married to Amelia, she sat there at the breakfast table with an enormous appetite. As they sat there, the nanny brought Clementine to them – so that she too could enjoy the celebration breakfast.

The new born was being fed a breakfast of milk in Clementine's room. William, Amelia and young Clementine sat in the dining room with the French windows open, the long lace curtains blowing out nearly touching the three of them, it was a wonderful day.

As much as William didn't want to on that warm, sunny day with a slight breeze – he had to go down to Ryde on business.

He stood up, touching hold of Amelia's hand, then kissing it, he told her that he wouldn't be late back. Amelia smiled, then William lent across the table, kissed Clementine, and made his exit.

That afternoon, when William had arrived home, and took up his usual role of playing with Clementine in the gardens, Amelia sat under the shade of her parasol, with the new born baby, just watching William. He looked happy to her, he looked happy with the children, but there was something she could see in his face, something that she just couldn't put her finger on. She decided at that moment, that that night she would have an in depth talk with him, and somehow try to find out what was going on in his head.

After the evening meal, the nanny relieved William and Amelia of the two children to get them ready for bed. Amelia asked William what was bothering him, as over the past few weeks, she could see a difference in him. He turned to her, and in-between sips of his brandy, told her that there was nothing bothering him, he was just simply longing for a baby boy. Amelia immediately went quite. He realised this, and re-assured her that it was only a case of a man who wanted a son for the sake of fishing and the other sports that men did, a thing that he himself had done with his father. Amelia's face softened at once, she rose from her seat, then walked across past the table and to the back of William's chair.

Putting her arms around his neck, then kissing him on the cheek, she muttered, "I'm sorry."

Four months later, William and Amelia were planning the Christening of their second child. The decided to call her Elizabeth.

After Elizabeth's christening, they held several more parties, although William seemed to Amelia, to be flirting with all the other young fillies at the parties. If she started to talk to anyone else, he became very possessive and jealous.

Two months after Elizabeth's christening, and after a violent row one evening, Amelia thought to herself that all that was going on was a stupid waste of time, it also wasn't doing any good for either of them, or the marriage. She tried the subtle approach towards William, which worked. They ended up that night together, a reminder of nights passed......

The morning after, William was extremely attentive towards Amelia, just as if there hadn't been a cross word between them.

Then over the next few months William started to behave like an animal towards Amelia. Approaching her at every opportunity. He seemed crazed in his obsession for a son. Soon enough, poor Amelia was once again pregnant.

She was happy with this knowledge, as she knew that it wouldn't be long before William would be back to his normal, caring self with her.

On the realisation that she was carrying his third child, and this one might be the son he desperately wanted, he did change. Once again he played with Clementine and Elizabeth. Once again, he was walking around the grounds of his small mansion with his loving wife and adoring children. What a sight for the surrounding neighbours to behold, as they had all noticed a drop in the family walks.

However, the toil of the past few months must have left its toll upon the servants, as the day before Amelia was due her third child, two of them left the service of the Browning family. It was said that they had received a post on the other side of the Island, which suited them better, although the reason for their sudden departure was never really known. The remaining servants in the Browning household were one full time maid and the children's nanny. One person who had stayed loyal to Amelia, was the midwife, and for the third time, she moved back into the

Browning house, so she could be near Amelia 24 hours a day.

The day the third child was born was a very tense day indeed. William retired to his study, but this time, he'd left his door slightly ajar, so that he could hear the servant who was attending the birth, and hear when the midwife called for him.

He skipped from book to book, not really looking at them, just waiting. The fire grate was cold, leaving a chill in the dark and depressing room. Although this was the third time William had found himself in this position, he still had that excited feeling in his stomach. He walked from book shelf to book shelf, across the room to stand at the window – it was windy that day and he couldn't take his eyes off the grass, and how the blades lent to one side. Standing there, staring in a semi day dream, he thought about Clementine and her younger sister playing there with there sun hats on. He could picture Amelia walking up to them pushing a perambulator with blue ribbons hanging from it, he smiled to himself, he felt content.

"Sir, *SIR!*" were the cries that abruptly broke him out of his daydream, and snapped him back to the reality of the moment. He quickly gathered himself together and spun round to find the last remaining servant stood in the door way.

"Sir," she said. "I'm so glad for you and milady"

"Thank you," he said as he rushed past her and headed straight for the staircase.

As he ran up the stairs reaching the top of the staircase, there was one hell of a holy CRACK! A tree branch came crashing through the window just to the left of him, a victim of the winds that were getting stronger and stronger by the hour. He span around, and there, at the bottom of the stairs was the servant.

"Clean it up!" he ordered, and proceeded to the room that Amelia was in.

As he walked into the room, he could hear the wind howling through the cracks of the windows and down the chimney. There was a fire burning, but the back draft kept giving of small wafts of smoke. The midwife was sat in one of the easy chairs near the fire, with a small bundle in her arms. There were no cries coming form it, just silence, only to be marred by the odd crack and spit from the logs in the fire grate.

Amelia lay on her stomach, exhausted, fast asleep. As he looked again at the midwife, he noticed that she had her head drooped. He walked across to her.

"Well," he said "is it alright?"

The midwife looked up at him, and with no emotion said, "I'm sorry, I'm truly *very* sorry."

He dropped his hand down, and laid it on the bundle that was in the midwife's arms. It was so still, it felt un-natural, solid – the child was dead. He took the child carefully out of the midwife's arms, and cradled it.

"What was it?" he asked quietly.

The midwife looked up, and with tears streaming down her cheeks, turned her head towards William, and sobbing said "Sir, it's the first baby I've ever lost........"

"Damn it woman! What was it!" William yelled at her.

"A, a boy Sir."

The words seemed to stick in his throat, he felt weak, like someone had just punched him in the stomach.

"Why! *WHY?!*" he sobbed as he fell to his knees, still cradling the baby in his arms.

"The one above only knows Sir," the midwife replied, as William just knelt there staring into the fire.

William started to cry, first tears rolling down his checks, then sobs, uncontrollable sobbing that shook his whole body and came straight from his heart.

The midwife gently took the child from William's trembling arms, she carried the child out of the room towards another room that would be much cooler than William and Amelia's bedroom.

William was still slumped there on his knees, his arms now straight down beside him, he was just staring into the fire. Slowly he turned his head and looked at Amelia. There she lay oblivious to what had gone on after the birth of the baby. She was laying there, lost in her dreams, dreams playing with Clementine and Elizabeth, but with one eye watching the perambulator which held the newest edition to the family, a chubby little William.

William's hopes had now been dashed. It was inconceivable in his mind that he had been so close, yet so far away from his dream, a dream of having a son, a son who would one day follow in his footsteps.

He rose from his knees, not giving Amelia a second glance, then walked straight out of the room and along the landing towards another room, a room that was furnished as a guest room when they used to have guests stay many months ago. Ripping off his clothes in a frenzy, he climbed into a very large, cold damp bed, and pulled the covers over himself. He shivered uncontrollably as he lay there with his head on the pillow staring at the window. Tears began to roll down his face. He could taste the salty fluid as it entered the corner of his mouth. Thought after thought convinced him that he now really **hated** Amelia, it was **her** fault that the child had died. She didn't want him to have a son, she was jealous, jealous of all the things that they could have shared as men. He quickly jumped out of the bed, and stepped into his trousers. He searched for the jacket he had flung somewhere in the room when he undressed. Grabbing a blanket from the bed he threw it about his shoulders, then stepped out of the room, and down the landing, kicking Amelia's door on his way to his study.

CHAPTER 8

The following morning, William woke to the birds twittering outside the study window. It was early, very early. He was cold, and as he lifted his head off the arm of one of the large winged chairs, it felt as if his neck was about to snap. He knew why he was there, and even though he'd been asleep, the last thoughts on his mind were that of the day before. He still felt the same, that it was **her** fault.

The midwife entered Amelia's room to see if she was all right, and to also break the news gently to her about her loss. As she opened the curtains, the sunlight shone brightly through the room. The beams of light hit one of the mirrors that hung on the wall, and illuminated the wall above Amelia's head. Amelia groaned then turned over to lay on her other side. As she was turning, she opened her eyes, catching a glimpse of the midwife.

"Good morning" she said smiling at the midwife. "How is my baby this beautiful morning?"

The midwife walked across the room to the side of the bed, and sat down slowly. She took hold of Amelia's hand. Sensing that something was not right, Amelia looked with concern at the midwife.

"There's something wrong isn't there?" she asked with a slight shake in her voice.

"Yes milady, there is."

"Tell me, **please,** tell me" Amelia said, trying to keep her voice calm.

The midwife explained to her that these things sometimes happened, and it was by no means a sign that it would ever happen again. Amelia just lay there staring at the ceiling. She felt no emotion what-so-ever, no tears rolled from her eyes, she felt numb.

"Where's William and the children?" she asked in a surprisingly cold voice.

"The children are with the nanny, and I think Mr Browning is in his study." replied the midwife.

"Help me up" Amelia requested.

"It's better that you rest madam," the midwife answered with concern growing inside her.

"Please, help me up."

This time Amelia's order was more forceful, and against her better judgement, the midwife helped her to get up and into her clothes.

William had closed the door to his study and locked it. He was now entombed there, licking his wounds, trying to come to terms with what had happened.

As Amelia reached the foot of the stairs, she glanced across to the tightly shut study door. She knew that William would be in there, but her main urgency was to see Clementine and Elizabeth.

She found them in one of the large drawing rooms with the nanny playing, oblivious to the whole situation. As Amelia walked in with the midwife close by her side, the children stopped playing. Leaving their nanny, they ran up to her and threw their arms around each of her legs. Amelia placed her hands upon their heads and gently ran her fingers through their hair. Two sets of arms immediately went up in the air, reaching to find the arms of their mother, to lift and embrace them. Alas, all Amelia could do was take them by the hand. She walked them across to one of the large easy chairs and sat down, gently positioning the children in front of her knees. As she talked to them, part of her mind was fixed on William, wondering what he was doing and how he was taking the situation.

A few hours later, William emerged from the study. His hair was all over the place, he sported a very dark shadowy look around his face, due to the fact he hadn't shaved for the past two days. Amelia handed the children back to the nanny, then followed William into the kitchen.

She found him sitting at one of the tables, arms stretched in front of him, and hands clasped. Amelia, without saying a word, reached for the bread, and took it to him. As she lay it down before him, she asked him what he would like with it. He just shrugged his shoulders, which told her he didn't care.

After a meal of bread and cheese, washed down with wine, he stood up and walked back to his study, but this time he didn't lock the door. Amelia thought that this would be the ideal time for them to talk, with the children being looked after the nanny, they could talk without distraction, about the previous night.

She entered the study and saw William sitting in a large winged chair, starring into the empty fire place. The tick of the mantle clock sounded exceptionally loud in the stillness of the room. She felt nervous, so nervous that she could have vomited. She walked towards him, and on passing him, she let her hand trail across his shoulders. Sitting down in the chair across form him, she spoke softly and gently, asking him to talk about how he felt. He looked at her and smiled, it wasn't a happy smile, but a sad one. Once again he told her that he would love a son and heir who could share his likings, and who would continue the family name, to keep the Browning estate safe.

Amelia turned her head to look out the window at the blue sky beyond. Slowly turning her head back. She looked at him, she started to smile. Carefully sliding off her chair and onto her knees, she took his hands in hers.

"We can try again" she whispered.

Two weeks went by, and William was executing his daily routine around the house, but the atmosphere was still strained. He seemed to start to withdraw within himself, and his mood changed drastically. Amelia had first noticed this the day that Elizabeth was born, but never mentioned it. She'd noticed, along with many people that used to visit them, that on showing them around the house, Elizabeth's room was decorated in blue, and William would always change the subject when it arose.

Ten months later, Amelia was pregnant for the fourth time. William for the last two months of her pregnancy, had slipped back to his excited self again. On the afternoon that she actually went into labour, he was pacing the hallway at the bottom of the stairs. Things for a while went quiet. He couldn't understand this, so he walked up the stairs and waited patently on the landing near the master bedroom. He sat down on one of the landing chairs, elbows in his knees, fiddling with his fingers. He could hear the long drawn out tick of the grand-father clock, ticking away as it had done for many a year before he was born.

At the strike of the old clock, William looked up – it was four o'clock. A child started to cry – a baby was born!

As he rushed into the room, there stood the usual midwife holding a tiny baby wrapped in torn sheets securely in her arms. The smile was now back on his face, the midwife was smiling too, knowing that she had once more brought another life into the world.

"Congratulations Mr Browning, you have a lovely baby girl. What are you going to call her?"

Amelia was laid there, with her head to one side on the pillow, half through exhaustion, and half awaiting his reaction. William slowly turned around and walked out of the room, down the stairs and back into his study. Amelia instantly knew that things from that day on, were not going to be right in the Browning household. Unless she could produce a boy, she knew her marriage would soon be over.

The midwife had by this time retired with the new born to clean her and put her to rest in the small crib.

The oil lamp was burning bright as it had been through the birth. Amelia turned her head, sating at the flame the flame that burnt within the glass prism. Her eyelids felt very heavy by now, the only thing that she felt, was that she had let William down, again. She knew that he would never forgive her for having another girl. The room was now quite dark with only the shadows from the flickering oil lamp dancing on the walls.

The wind had risen drastically making the fire crack and spit even more. She tried hard to understand why William was acting this way towards her, when many families found it hard to have children, families who would have given their soul to have what they had.

A solitary tear rolled down her face, she thought of when she was child, curled up in bed, feeling safe. Thoughts of her children and her husband were so distant that they didn't matter. She thought of the dreams she'd had when she was small, dreams of her perfect family – a loving husband and children, happy laughing children. Suddenly her thoughts were shattered, and reality hit her, what had gone wrong with her life? Why her?!

Just at that moment the midwife walked back into the room, and straight to where Amelia was laid. She sat down at the side of her placing her hand upon Amelia's head.

"Don't worry." the midwife said trying to re-assure Amelia. "He doesn't understand."

Amelia slid across the bed closer to the midwife, it was as if she was sliding towards her mother for comfort. The mother she hadn't seen for *so* many years, because her family had moved across the water to the mainland. Amelia just lay there, seeking comfort, anybody's comfort would have done just at that moment, she was so mixed up, self pity overtook, and she found that she didn't give a damn about anyone else.

The midwife rose from the bed, telling Amelia to get her rest, and that she would see her in the morning, unless she needed anything during the night. Amelia slumped back into the large soft pillows. They seemed to wrap themselves a quarter way around her face, giving her maximum comfort.

CHAPTER 9

The morning after, Amelia woke to the sunlight beaming through her bedroom window. The only thing on her mind was to see her children, Clementine, Elizabeth and the new born – which had yet to be named. She slowly slid out of bed, still feeling pain from the previous day's ordeal, but that didn't matter as long as she could see her children.

Once dressed, she walked towards the stairway to take on the long descent, step by step she slowly placed one foot down before the other, clutching the handrail as she went. Once at the foot of the stairs, she could hear the children playing outside, giggling together, then the occasional scream. As she reached the front door – which was wide open and letting in the crisp air – she could see the children playing on the grass under the ever watchful eye of the nanny. The nanny was sat on the third step from the bottom, gently rocking the perambulator. As she watched the happy sight, she knew that William would never be the same again, and that she would devote her life totally to her children.

As the weeks rolled on, Amelia could be seen taking long walks with the children, around the grounds of the house. She would take secretive glances at the study window, and often catch William peeping through the curtains. He had not spoken to her, or slept with her since the birth of the last daughter.

During the evenings, Amelia sat alone in the drawing room, either needle-pointing or reading. She could hear William leaving his study and head for the kitchens. She would sit there frozen, holding her breath, waiting to hear if this time, the door of the drawing room would open. But, it never did.

Two months had quickly flown by. The weather had changed to gloomy days and dark early nights. Amelia was now practically a prisoner in the house that she'd once loved.

One night, after retiring early with a book, Amelia lay in bed staring at the images dancing on the walls, made by the flames of the oil lamp. The door handle started to turn slowly. She quickly turned her head, her heart pounding, as she lay there frozen. The door slowly opened, and there stood William, just in his shirt and trousers. He walked across the room towards her, not speaking a word. He was unshaven and dirty looking, but to Amelia, he was a welcome sight, no matter how he looked.

He undid his shirt buttons and slid off his trousers, he laid them on the bed, Amelia just lay there breathing fast, her chest heaving in and out. With one hand he pulled back the sheets, and climbed in the bed beside Amelia.

There was no sweet talk, no kisses. He acted like a paid for bull at a stud farm. Amelia held him tightly, trying to pretend that nothing was wrong between them, that everything was like it used to be. She still loved him dearly.

He left just as quickly as he'd arrived – still without speaking a word.

After that night, Amelia had the baby christened, she'd named her Violet. The nanny, although still working for the Browning's, had herself cut down the number of hours that she worked, due to problems of her own. This threw more days of solitude onto Amelia.

The weeks went on and on, William had 'visited' Amelia in her room, twice more, and still without any emotion. Amelia was practically bringing up three children on her own, and the pressures were starting to take their toll.

She would only see William for a few minutes each day, as he would retreat rapidly after his days business, like a wisp of air, into his study. By now Amelia was looking tired, haggard and drawn – a far cry from that beautiful young woman who had once danced in the large splendid ballroom.

She started to feel ill and depressed with the continuous mornings of being sick. Knowing full well her symptoms, she decided it was time to see the Browning's family doctor, who after two examinations, confirmed what she already knew and dreaded – she was pregnant, again!

This time, she was determined not to say anything to William, she just simply wanted to have the baby, then, if it was a boy, this would be the re-birth of their marriage. The one thing she had to do, was keep away from William, keep away form his periodical visits, and hope that on her routine travels around the house and gardens, he didn't notice anything.

One morning the nanny had just arrived and took the children to one of the drawing rooms, giving Amelia a full day of relaxation. As she sat in the kitchen, drinking a cup of tea, thinking how wonderful it was not to have to worry, where, and what the two older girls were doing, there was a sudden banging on the front door, Amelia looked up at the wall clock – it was 9.30a.m.

Who on earth could this be, she wondered as she made her way to the front door. As she opened the door, there was a young boy standing there. In his hand, he held a letter, a special delivery that had just come through from the mainland. As he handed the letter to Amelia, he stood there staring at her, still not saying a word. Amelia stared back, wondering what she'd done, she'd seen this look before with other people. She suddenly realised, that the boy was waiting for a tip. She told him to wait, closed the door, hurried down the hall and into the kitchen. She looked for the small tin which had coins in for the purpose of paying tradesmen. Still clutching the letter, she reached for the tin and pulled out a farthing to give to the boy.

When she opened the front door, the boy was still waiting patiently, he began to smile, he knew that within seconds, he would be wealthy for that day, and that he could buy all the sweets that he wanted.

"Thanks ma'am" he said as she handed him the coin, he doffed his cap, then quickly spun around and ran off.

Amelia walked back towards the kitchen, wondering who had written to her after all these years! She sat down with the letter in her hands, staring at it, frightened to open it, yet at the same time, thrilled with the contact it meant with the outside world.

She walked across to the old stone sink, and there, left on the side was a very worn down potato knife. Picking it up, she slipped it under the lip of the envelope, and slashed it open. She let the knife fall to the floor, she was intrigued as to what the contents could be. With her hands shaking, she slid the letter out of the envelope and unfolded it. She could see that it had come form a mainland solicitor.

In a very official and sympathetic legal way, the letter told her there had been a tragic accident involving her parents, and that they had both been killed. Amelia fell to her knees, clutching the letter to her chest, her mouth wide open. She felt winded, tears began to roll from her eyes.

She couldn't move, it was like every muscle in her body had given up.

With the help of the sink, she slowly managed to pull her-self up, still clutching the letter. On shaky legs, bumping into things, through the tears that were burning her face, and blurring her vision, she slowly walked from the kitchen to her room. A room of loneliness, a house of emptiness, a life of – God only knew!

As she reached her bed, she fell forwards on her stomach, sobbing uncontrollably, wondering who was going to take care of the children while she attended her parents funeral on the mainland. After a short time, tiredness form the sobbing overwhelmed her, and she fell into a troubled sleep.

Sometime later, she woke to the chimes of the mantle clock. She got herself up and walked out of the room, along the landing to William's rooms. Knocking gently on the door, and calling his name softly, she opened the door, hinges creaking with every movement. Nervously peeping around the door, she scanned the room for William, but he wasn't there. He was still in his study. Gently closing the door again, she turned and started to walk down the stairs and to the study. She tried to get some order in her head about the news she'd received, and that she wanted to ask William to look after the children, while she went to the mainland.

After knocking on the study door, she opened it slowly. There was William, sat on a chair near the window, starring out, as if he was watching a play at one of the island's theatres. Still unsteady on her feet, she walked over to him, and placed her hand on his shoulder. He sat there motionless. Amelia felt as if she had placed her hand on one of the boulders in the flower beds of the garden.

After what seemed like a life-time to Amelia, he slowly turned his head towards her, there was no smile, not even a twitch at the corner of his lips. His face looked drawn and grey. He had dark circles around his eyes, and his eyes gave off an insane stare.

Amelia was afraid to speak, wondering what his reaction would be towards her. Would he shout at her? Would he ignore her? Or, would he beat her?

Plucking up courage, she softly spoke his name. Still clutching the letter, she held out her hand, trying with all her might to stop it from shaking.

"William," she said "I must go to the mainland. Would you take care of the children please."

"No" he replied flatly. "They belong to you. Your place is here with them. You **do not** leave this house."

"But, but my parents have been killed." she said, trying unsuccessfully to control the shakiness in her voice, and stop the tears rolling down her face. "I must attend their funeral."

"We all have to die." he replied callously. "Now leave me woman."

Amelia turned and walked out of the study. As she closed the door she fell back against it. She could hardly believe what she had just heard. She just stood there, her head a tangled mass of emotions. One thing was clear to her, and that was she now knew that she was a prisoner of Williams clutches, that she would have to adhere to everything that he said. Still she stood there, hoping against hope that her would come after her and would have changed his mind, but nothing. His word was final.

CHAPTER 10

Amelia's weeks of toil went on. She spent her days walking in the gardens and looking after the children. She wrote a letter to her brothers and sisters on the mainland, making her apologies and excuses for not attending her parents' funeral – but not one word in that letter blamed William for her not being able to attend.

William still visited her occasionally, but on his visits, she just lay there motionless. The days of pretending that they were still in love, were well over.

When Amelia started to show that she was pregnant, William noticed, but still did not say anything to her. His visits grew less and less, until they stopped all together a month before she was due to have the baby.

The midwife was on standby once again, but had agreed weeks previous, to assist at the Browning household, only until Amelia was back on her feet, and able to look after the children. In the state of mind Amelia was in, she was only too happy to agree to these terms. She appreciated any sort of rest from the children and anyone who was there – no matter for how brief a period – was company for her. The situation she was in now, was a far cry from the old days. No loving husband, no visits from so called friends, no outings, and to top it all, the servants were starting to pity her.

The day of the birth came. Amelia couldn't rest at all, she had to keep walking just to ease the back pain. Eventually, she had to retreat to her room, then finally to the bed. The pans were on the boil in the kitchen, sheets were being torn, and the nanny was running around trying very hard to keep the children under control and quiet for Amelia, but most of all because of William.

Periodically the study door would creek open and stay ajar, until there was a sign of people near, then it would be angrily slammed shut.

Amelia's labour had started, and to the midwife, it did not look good at all. In fact, for the first time in her career, the midwife was becoming more and more concerned for Amelia's well being. At eight thirty that night, Amelia still hadn't given birth, and was rapidly becoming weaker and weaker with each contraction. The midwife immediately called the nanny, and instructed her with all speed to get the doctor. The nanny grabbed a shawl form the back of the nearest chair, and dashed through the door. The midwife heard the front door bang shut, and prayed to herself that the doctor would arrive in time.

As the doctor arrived, he lunged through the front door, throwing his cape onto the hall table, and with great speed – still clutching his Gladstone bag – ran up the stairs and into Amelia's room. The second he saw her, he knew that there was no time to waste, and that she must have the baby soon, or he would loose them both. Within minutes, the nanny walked into the room, carrying two large kettles of boiling water, after placing them where the doctor had directed, she turned around, and slowly she closed the large oak bedroom door.

All the upstairs landing was silent. Down stairs in the hall, the doctors cape slowly slid off the table and onto the floor. The tick of the old grandfather clock carried on with its rhythmic pattern, just as it had always done. The study was in darkness, with just one beam of moonlight illuminating the chair by the window that William usually sat, but there was no William. He was leaning against the study door, with his ear pressed hard against it, listening for any sound he could pick up.

The sound of his heart beat pounded in his head. The top of his ear ached with being pressed so hard on the door. He moved his head fractionally from side to side, searching for maximum comfort and hearing.

The large oak door to Amelia's room opened, and out onto the landing walked the doctor rolling down his sleeves. The fight with the jaws of death was over, he'd won. As the nanny sat in front of the log fire holding the tiny infant, the midwife followed the doctor onto the landing.

"What do you think?" the midwife asked.

"I think she's going to need a lot of rest and care," the doctor replied. "I'll call back on a couple of days, unless there are any complications."

The doctor looked back into the room, and to the bed that Amelia was laying in. She looked so pale and small, he was so angry. As he walked down the landing, then down the stairs, he was putting his jacket on. Walking past the hall table, he bent down and picked his cape up form the floor. As he straightened up, and started for the front door, he stopped at the study. He wanted to go into the study and punch William straight in the mouth. Instead he angrily threw his cape around his shoulders, and walked out of the Browning house, slamming the door as he left.

William sensed by the footsteps pausing outside the study, and the slamming of the front door, that he'd not only lost a doctor, but a trusted and faithful friend.

The midwife walked from the landing back into Amelia's room and across to the nanny.

"Could you please take the child into your room tonight, and keep a careful eye on her?" she asked the nanny.

The nanny immediately rose from the chair, cradling the child in her arms. As she neared the door, she stopped, and turning round looked at the midwife then asked, "will milady be all right?"

"Yes" the midwife simply stated with a smile.

After the nanny had left, the midwife sat down on the bed beside Amelia and took hold of her hand, and prayed silently to herself. She spent the next three days sat on the bed beside Amelia, and the nights sleeping on a chair that she pulled to the bed. She left the room only when nature required her to, or to take empty plates to the kitchen. On the fourth day of her convalescing, Amelia was anxious to leave her bed and carry on her duties as a mother and a wife to a ghost husband.

The doctor had called on the second day of Amelia's confinement, to find her sleeping. On the report form the midwife, he decided to leave it a full week before visiting her again.

The nanny was feeling bad at having cut down her hours at the Browning house, and half blamed herself for Amelia nearly losing the baby's and her own life.

On the fifth morning, Amelia rose from her bed, dressed and then for a constant two hours, walked around the bedroom, until she thought that she was ready once more to take on life.

The doctor, true to his word, called back after a week. Amelia who had been out of bed for two days, felt pretty strong, and had started playing with the children again. The morning that the doctor called, Amelia was in the drawing room.

"How are you this morning?" the doctor asked.

"Fine doctor, thank you. I'm full of the joys of spring."

"I must stress one thing to you Amelia," the doctor said, in a stern, important voice. "You must **not** have anymore children, or there could be great consequences. Amelia it will endanger your life, not to mention the baby's."

"Doctor," she said flatly, "I can't promise that. You know very well William wants a son."

"William be hanged!" the doctor answered angrily through clenched teeth. "He should think himself lucky that he's got children at all!"

After he had explained all the complications that could arise if Amelia had any more children, he bade her a good day, and left. To Amelia, it was silly warning her of might-bes, those she simply didn't want to know. The doctor didn't understand, she had to have a boy, for William's sake. She wasn't concerned about herself, but she was William's wife and despite everything she loved him.

Shortly after the birth, the fourth child was christened. She was named Emily.

Over the years, William was often seen around the house, but he was still distant, and he never accepted the four girls as his. Amelia brought the four children up, and with the nanny long gone, had learnt to cope a little better.

William's visits to her bed carried on, and after the birth of three more daughters – Victoria, Agness and Charlotte – William's chances of Amelia ever giving birth to a son and heir, were finally over.

CHAPTER 11

That night, was the birth of all births, the sort that all families dread. William, as usual, had his ear pressed tightly to the door of the study. This must be the end to all his anxieties, she was surely going to have a boy, a boy that would look like him, a boy he could play with in his early years, and eventually carry on his family name.

There was the midwife, a nanny, plus the faithful old family doctor, all sharing the same concern. They knew by now, what Amelia wanted, and that if she had a boy, her life would be turned around in the eyes of William.

There they stood in Amelia's room, each and everyone of them doing their part. Everything was right, the water that had been boiled was waiting. The sheets torn, everything ready, right down to the large log fire burning in the grate.

William that night was experiencing a feeling that he'd never had before. A feeling that this time, after all the past attempts of becoming a real father to a son, that **this** time was to be the last time, that this time, he was going to have a son. He walked away from the study door for a while in order for him to bend his neck to ether side of his body, to crack and relieve the tension. Suddenly, he heard a cry of a difference, it was Amelia she was crying out for him, and only him.

"I love you, I love you William" he heard her cry so loudly.

"I........."

This was different! He flung the doors of the study open and ran up the stairs towards Amelia's room. As he ran up the stairs, he was thinking to himself, that this time she really had done it, he was thrilled with himself, and could not help giving little smirks to himself, at how clever he was. A boy he thought, at last, a boy!

As he burst through the door of Amelia's room, there stood the midwife, with a tiny bundle in her arms – a sight he had seen for the past seven births. But this time the midwife wasn't smiling. He stopped, stunned with surprise, she'd done it, he thought, she's done it. Then he glanced over to Amelia for her reaction.

There she lay, so restful after her ordeal. She had a look about her, a look that said she'd found the key to the hardest puzzle of her life. He slowly turned his head, bringing the midwife and the small bundle that she held in her arms, into full vision. The midwife was standing there rocking from side to side. Tears running down her cheeks, tears that seemed to build up on her jaw bone then drop to the ground – like the dew from the morning flowers.

William swiftly swung his head back towards the bed and Amelia. She looked *so* happy, so *young.* The haggard look had left her. She'd done it, it was a boy. He was convinced of that now, but he couldn't understand why the midwife was crying? Were those tears of happiness?

He glanced over to Amelia again. Her eyes were closed, her hand lay slightly to one side on the silk pillows, her hair was draped over the pillows, like it had been arranged for a photograph. She lay there with her arms out of the covers, her hands, one on top of the other, resting on her stomach. *She was DEAD!*

As the midwife walked out of the room with the last baby that Amelia would ever see, she paused for a second, looking William straight in the face.

"You'll never hurt her again!" she hissed at him.

As the door of Amelia's room closed for what would be one of the last times, William just stood there looking at her, knowing that all his sulkiness, and moodiness didn't matter any-more. This was real, permanent. In a few days time, he would never see the face of the woman he'd fallen in love with, the one he'd married – till death us do part.......
He heard the words growing soft as they trailed off in his mind.

There she lay, the body of the only person in William's life who had ever *really* loved him. And now, now she was gone. The person who had put up with his moods, his tantrums when things hadn't gone right, when his children had aches and pains, that he didn't want to know, but she was always there for him. All the things they had planned to do together when they were first married on those early mornings when they were too happy to sleep. All that was left now was a shell, there were no more thoughts, no more giggles, no more emotion. All he had used her for over the past few years was a baby machine to give him his *'precious'* son. It was too late now, he'd woken up to himself, but it was too late.

Sat by the fire was the nanny, her elbows on her knees, head in her hands and sobbing, uncontrollable sobs. The doctor walked towards William, rolling down his sleeves. He stopped suddenly at the side of him. William turned his head towards the doctor and just stared into his eyes, giving off a look of what am I going to do now my dear friend? The doctor turned away and picked up his jacket as he walked to the door and out of the room, quickly followed by the nanny.

There William stood, all alone in the same room as Amelia. A thing that he had done for years, only this time, Amelia couldn't slip down onto her knees, clasp his hand and tell him that they could try again. He walked across to the bed and stood there gazing at her face, wishing that he could turn back time.

Walking across the room towards the great log fire, he picked up the bowl of water that the doctor, the midwife and the nanny had used for washing their hands, he picked it up and flung it with all his might across the room. Turning the oil lamp down, he himself walked out the room.

CHAPTER 12

On the morning of the funeral, everything had been arranged. Everyone, but the children were allowed to attend. By this time, Clementine was old enough to watch over the other six children, and William made sure she did.

That morning, William, with his large black coat on, walked down the stairs to the front door to leave for the funeral. Clementine, with all her sisters, were waiting at the bottom of the stairs in a line – apart from the new born which Clementine had closely hugged in her arms. Their father stopped in front of them all, glaring at them with his dark piercing eyes.

"I'll be away at your mothers funeral for a while. Now make sure that your good. It's down to you Clementine."

"Yes father" she replied.

The children, all pale faced, just stood there with bated breath, watching every foot-step that he took, until the large front door banged shut behind him. Still they waited, until one of them thought they heard the large garden gates squeak. Clementine turned around to them all and said, "you all heard what father said, we must be good."

As Clementine turned around and walked into one of the large drawing rooms to lay the newborn down on one of the large winged chairs, the rest of the children were off, off like a pack of rats swarming all over the furniture, from room to room they went. They had never seen such things in their lives. Amelia had always been careful to keep them on a tight leash, so as not to disturb William.

Clementine, making sure that the newest addition to the family was fast asleep, closed the door to the drawing room.

"Shush!" she warned, as two of her younger sisters ran by, "the baby's asleep."

The two sisters stopped in their tracks. Then slowly started to walk by, only to burst into full speed again at the first door, then they vanished. There were shouts and cries from all over the house, but Clementine slowly walked upstairs and headed for her mothers room. A room that she'd spent many a frightened night in when she was younger. As she approached the room, she could hear that the rest of the children were slowly making their way upstairs to explore all the other rooms.

As she opened the door to the room, she paused and looked up and down the landing. The old grandfather clock struck its usual half hour beat. She carried on through, and into the bedroom. Closing the door behind her, she noticed that it felt cold. Her eyes drifted towards the fire place that looked dismal and cold, then across the room and finally onto the bed. The bed that once held her mama.

The curtains were closed, but she could still see the day light through them. She walked across towards the bed. Her love for her mother was so great that she just had to touch the blankets. Sitting down on the bed she could hear the other children shouting each other's names, and the the odd scream, but this was her time, the time that she would never have again – and she knew it.

Resting back gently, then turning onto her side, she lay her head down upon the silk pillow. She could smell the sweet perfume of her mother. It wasn't just perfume, it was the smell of her mama. The smell that lingered in her mind from when she was a baby, that certain smell that you relate to those you love. Her eyes filled with water, then tears began to roll down her cheeks, then she began sobbing, she held the sheets close to her mouth to muffle the sound of her hurt and pain.

In those few minutes, Clementine seemed to age by six years. She knew now that down stairs was a small life that needed her, just as much as she needed her mother.

As she rose from the bed, she had great difficulty in letting go of the sheets. She walked towards the door of her mother's room, she gave one last look at the bed where her mother had finally departed from this life.

As she opened the door, she knew that would be the last time she would ever see the room while her father was alive.

When she reached the bottom of the stairs, her father was just closing the front door behind him. All the other children must have heard him several minutes before she had but being involved in the games they were playing, didn't bother to shout her. They all stood in line. One had even been in the drawing room and collected the new born, whom she held tight in her arms.

Clementine slowly walked across the hall and stood directly in front of her sisters. She didn't know what to expect, it was either a slap across her face, or a damned good telling off. William walked down from the front door, taking off the long, dark overcoat, and stood directly in front of Clementine. There they stood, all six of them, looking hungry, hair uncombed with pale faces.

"Where have you been?" William yelled at Clementine.

"No-where father." she replied.

"Right, gather your sisters together, I want to talk to you all." he ordered before storming off to his study.

Clementine took hold of the baby, and walked into the drawing room with all her sisters following her. She sat in one of the large winged chairs with Charlotte in her arms. The rest cuddled around her feet. Minutes later, William walked back into the room with a face like thunder. There they all were, all the children sat huddled at the feet of Clementine, all shaking and trembling, not daring to make a move. Every one of their little pasty faces, with wide open eyes watching every move that this person, their father made. Their father was somebody they had only ever seen passing through the kitchen for food. Never had those big hands and strong arms lifted them, or patted them lovingly on the head. To the children, this man was the monster that lived behind the study doors. But now, he was standing in front of them, left hand holding the lapel of his jacket, right hand slung out in front of him, thumb looped into his waistcoat pocket.

He eventually sat down in the chair opposite Clementine and her sisters. This was his family, all he had left of Amelia now that she was gone. He just sat there and stared at them, not at all like a normal father would act towards his children, after just losing their mother. There would be the occasional sniffle from one of the children, then in a stern voice he said, "your mother has gone, so that means that all of you now have to pull your weight. I intend to keep you on the straight and narrow. You will have your chores to do, with the exceptions of Charlotte, Agnes and Victoria."

With that, he stood up and left for his study, where he made out a list of all the groceries that they would require through the week. Everything from the food that they ate, down to what would be required for the baby.

Before he left the house to go and collect the groceries, he looked around the corner of his door and into the room that he had left the children in. The look was enough, they were all still in the same positions as he'd left them in.

Once again the front door banged shut, and he was off. He decided to make the grocery list into a standing order, and requested that it be left on the top step of the main entrance to the house every week, telling them to send the account to him at the end of every three months.

The minute William had left, the children were all off again in different directions, but this time Clementine shouted them back, not in a little girls voice, but a much sterner, meaningful mothers voice. She knew that she must, at all times, keep her sisters from running riot.

Once they were all standing around her once again, she started to explain that if they did as she asked them, they would start to have a better life even though mama was gone. Clementine walked in to the kitchen with the small baby in her arms, as Charlotte was getting very hungry. The other children began to play hide and seek, hunger not entering their minds for one minute. They darted from one room to another, snuggling under tables and chairs, and hiding in any dark corner that they thought they might not be seen. But slowly hunger got the better of them, and one after another they slowly started to wonder into the kitchen until they were all seated around a huge pine table with a chunk of bread clutched in one hand, and a piece of cheese in the other.

The door banged again, and the children froze, two or three of them dropped their bread. Their father walked into the kitchen, followed by a young man carrying a basket of groceries. The young man walked straight to the end of the large table, and without even looking up, unloaded the basket, then he left. It appeared he had been warned not, for one minute, to cast his eyes on anything or anybody in that room.

Clementine got up and passed Charlotte to one of the older girls, then walked towards her father and stood by his side.

"See it away." he said in a stern voice. "I see you have all had your meals." Then he walked out of the kitchen and straight into his study. With one loud **bang!** The door was closed and Clementine knew from past experience with her mother, that would be the last time they would see him until the following morning.

It was starting to get dark outside, and she knew that she had to concentrate on all the children being in one of the many bedrooms, and get plenty of candles there, so that she could be on hand for any of them during the night. She hurriedly looked through the drawers for candles, finally finding mounds of them in one of the pantries that had been used by the servants in the earlier years. She quickly shunted her sisters one by one up the stairs, knowing that once they were all in one room, and with some carefully chosen bedding, they would be safe.

Once the girls were in the bedroom, Clementine ran down the stairs and quickly filled a large jug with cold water, knowing that if one of her sisters woke during the night for a drink, she would have it ready. She also took with her some fresh milk for the newborn. This was the start to a ritual that would carry on, not only for that night, but for several nights, leading into months, until they had become organised as a small family team.

CHAPTER 13

Over the following months, the seven girls hardly saw their father, only the odd shouts or muddled speech, from a person who had had too much brandy.

When Charlotte, the youngest of the seven was three, Clementine, with the rest of her sisters, was practically running the house. They never saw their father, but they knew that behind the study door, he was there sitting after his nocturnal habits, or after a hurried visit to the kitchen. They all knew they had to be extremely quiet during the day, but with a little cunningness, they could get away, with Clementine's permission, with anything they wanted. The garden and the house became their whole world. They didn't know what it would be like to leave the grounds and venture out into the big wide world.

Many a day, Clementine and Elizabeth would be standing at the old stone sink washing, when one of the children would run up to them with some sort of problem, or some sort of daring task that wanted Clementine's permission to act out.

After the evening meal, the same old questions were asked of Clementine, "what was it like outside the iron gates?" Of course she couldn't answer them honestly - she'd never been out there, but she did her best by making up stories for them. A different story each night, but all with the same warning of how evil it was out there. The children would sit there with open mouths, large glaring eyes, and gasping for breath, picturing all the evils that took place beyond the gates.

Many a night, the stories would be halted by the coughing that came from the study. The scared thoughts of being able to walk out of the gates, was nothing compared to the one's they had of behind that door.

One day as Clementine was preparing vegetables for the rest of the children, Violet quickly walked up behind her. Clementine dropped the peeling knife into the sink, and turned to her sister to see what was wrong.

" Clementine," Violet started.

"Yes Violet" answered Clementine.

"Would it be all right if we had a cat?"

"No Violet, we can't be doing with any animals while father is as he is." Clementine answered sadly.

Violet looked up at her sister, with big pleading eyes, and carefully, from under the covers of her little wicker basket, she produced the sweetest little kitten that you could ever imagine. Clementine looked at its little face, which as if on cue, gave her a soft me-ow, and a look of 'who's going to look after me now?' Clementine knew that feeling only to well after her mother had died, she felt exactly the same way as the kitten before her. She took the kitten from Violet, and as she was holding it in both hands, it started to rub its head on her hands and wrist. It started to me-ow constantly, it was like a plea for help. Its lost, I'm lost, we are all lost, she thought to herself. She lifted the kitten to her face and gently kissed it.

"Yes little fellow, you can stay."

She then placed the kitten on the floor, and poured out the remains of the chilled milk. It made her feel good watching the kitten drink milk. She knew that she and all her sisters would make the kitten feel loved, a feeling that they had once felt with their mother. Clementine had the final decision – the cat stayed! But where was the cat food going to come from? How were they going to conceal it from father? Clementine made a few adjustments to the grocery order. Firstly she ordered one pound of fish a day, and if this was ever noticed by father, she had made a story up saying she felt sorry for a stray cat. If their father ever did find out, then the girls would just save the cat scraps from their meals – though they ate simply. Not one of the girls knew how to cook, partly as they had no-one to teach them, and also ladies of their stature simply didn't do that sort of thing.

The years marched on, and the cat had kittens and the kittens had kittens. Over all this time, Clementine – who by now was leaving the grocery order herself in the empty basket – had started adding to the list extra amounts of food for the cats, until eventually every Friday morning, there were one hundred cans of cat food being delivered, along with the other groceries.

It soon became apparent that the seven sisters were losing their sanity, as was their father, who 2 years previous had ordered a magazine. This had been delivered weekly over those years, but nobody in the

60

household had settled the account for the last six months. A debt collector had to be called in. As he walked up the long stairs of the back entrance towards the back door, he got a strange feeling that things were not as they should be.

After knocking on the door and waiting for several minutes (he dare not come away without a payment as he feared it would result in the loss of his job) the door slowly opened, and one of the sisters appeared. The collector noticed that the rolled magazines were stacked unopened all the way down the long dark passage. There were so many, that they had spilled over onto the pathway towards the back door, and they had been flattened by foot with out being removed. William by this time was in very poor health. He would put his name to practically anything that Clementine asked. Clementine was the only one who had permission to enter his study to settle accounts, but every time she went there, she felt uneasy. Partly because after all the years, she still didn't know him properly, and also she didn't know if he was re-arranging his weekly grocery list. She would often think to herself, while she stood waiting for the cash or a note of approval, would it be today that he notices the deception which the girls were carrying out every day, the feeding of the cats, or the walking in the grounds but he never did. The debt collector was paid in full and the magazine cancelled.

Alas, the time came, when after years of suffering, their father passed away. It was one early morning that Clementine had to enter the study for the weekly food cheque. The other six sisters were about their morning chores. Clementine, as usual, opened the study door very slowly and carefully, but this particular day, she sensed that something was amiss. The whole study was in complete darkness, the curtains were still drawn, and the mantle clock had stopped. She walked across the room and swiftly opened the curtains. There was William, sat in one of the large winged back chairs.

"Father" she said. "Father, I need the cheque for the groceries."

As she reached his side, she could see the whiteness of his face, his eyes were wide open, his jaw slightly dropped. She stood there motionless for a while. She knew that he had passed away, it was the same expression as her mother had, even though she'd only seen her for a short while after she'd died. Slowly dropping to her knees at the side of her father, she placed her hand onto his, feeling the cold, solid feel of a dead person. She just knelt there, staring at his face. A single tear ran down her face, as she remembered the days playing in the garden with him. Those were days of happiness, seeing him smile, then catching a glimpse of her mother laughing. As she sat there lost in her thoughts, she wondered what had ever happened to her parents, what had happened to make them both so unhappy. Clementine brought herself back to reality, and rising from her knees, she walked across to the curtains, and closed them. She then calmly walked out of the room to inform her sisters of what had just happened.

She gathered them all together, and in a soft, gentle voice told them that their father was dead. There they all stood, just in the same position as they had done many years before when they were children, but this time they were young women. Not one of them showed any emotion what-so-ever, as it had always been up to Clementine to have the dealings with their father.

The morning after, Clementine rose very early and walked to the large iron gates at the bottom of the garden. She knew that was the day the groceries were to be delivered, and that she must get a message to the family doctor via the small delivery boy. As she waited, face pressed against the bars, she listened to the chirps and caws of the birds. Several cats by this time were swirling in and around her feet, jut rubbing themselves against her legs, then slipping through the gates, and off towards a day of excitement. How could they do that? What was out there? Where they not frightened? She gazed at them slipping away one by one, down the lane to where? Why couldn't she do it? Why!

Just at that moment, slowly but surely, there trudged the old cart horse, pulling the flat cart loaded with several peoples' orders in boxes up the lane. It eventually stopped at the side of the garden gates of the Browning estate. The young lad jumped down and around to the side nearest the gates.

"It's heavy Miss," he said, dragging the large box off the side of the cart. "Do you want me to help you up to the house?" hoping all the time that Clementine would say yes.

"No, thank you" Clementine said, "I have enough sisters to help me."

"Please yourself Miss," he said dragging the box over towards the gates. As he left it there, he turned and headed back to his horse and cart.

"Young man," Clementine called after him, "here's a farthing, would you please ask the Brownings doctor to call as soon as possible?"

"Is there someone ill?" asked the young boy, knowing that any information he could find out about the family, would make him the most popular person for the week. As she did not reply, he walked back towards the gates holding out his hand, then eventually clasping the farthing in his sweaty little palm, he said, "Sure I'll do that for you Miss. I suppose I will see him when I drop his order at his house later today."

"Thank you." Clementine replied. "You are very kind." she turned around and walked back towards the house for the help from her sisters.

The six of them soon scurried down the pathway towards the large box that held their food and the hundred tins of cat food. They didn't need to be told twice by Clementine to do something.

Later that day, as Clementine was sat on the opposite chair to her father's in his study doing some needlework, she would occasionally look up at her father, as if there had never been any unusual behaviour by him, she suddenly heard a tapping of a stick on the front door. Carefully placing her needlework on the seat that she had risen from, she walked out of the study and to the front door.

There stood at the door, and just about to open it stood Emily.

"I'll get it Emily." Clementine said.

As she opened the door, there stood the doctor.

"You wished to see me Clementine." he said.

"Yes doctor. Would you please come with me." she said, as she walked towards the study.

"Wait." she said, then walked across to the curtains, and flung them open.

The doctor scanned the room, and immediately saw William sat in one of the chairs. He walked across to him with haste.

"Clementine, he is dead." The doctor could hardly believe his own words.

"Yes doctor I know, that's why I sent for you. What do we do now? You know that my sisters and I cannot leave the house, we are too frightened." she stated matter of factly.

"Come Clementine," the doctor replied.

"No doctor," she interrupted. "You must make all the necessary arrangements, and then when it's all over, I will pay you in full for your time and trouble."

The doctor stood there amazed. What has all these years of captivity done to these children, he thought. He looked at the floor, then slowly lifted his eyes until he was looking directly into Clementine's piercing eyes. She was so cold, so hollow, like a shell without a soul.

"I shall take care of it." he said. He slowly took his eyes from hers. "I'll be back to you within the hour," he said as he slowly walked out of the room, and closed the door.

Clementine walked back towards the winged back chair. She picked up her needlework and sat down. She just held it in her hands staring at her father. She wanted only to be with him for those last minutes, like he had been with her when she was small.

True to his word, within the hour the doctor was back with two more men. Victoria had let them in, and as they were about to enter the study, Clementine walked out. She knew that her place was now at the side of her sisters. She was the only person that they had left. It was a good half hour before she heard the front door close. As she walked out of the drawing room and into the hall, the doctor was standing there. "Is everything done doctor?" she asked.

"Yes Clementine, your father has left now. I will be in touch with you about the funeral service, where and when it will be held."

"Thank you doctor."

The doctor turned and walked out of the house, still not fully believing what he had just witnessed.

As Clementine re-entered the drawing room, the rest of her sisters where just sitting around in different chairs, all bar one of them – Charlotte. She was standing at the window, staring out onto the lawn and pathway that lead to the large iron gates.

"Are you all right Charlotte?" asked Clementine placing her hand on her sister's shoulder.

"Yes." She said, "I was just wondering which one of us will be taking that journey next Clementine" she said hesitantly, "what's it like out there?"

Clementine simply hugged her.

"Come, we have things to do," was the only reply Clementine was going to give.

A few days later, the doctor was back at the house to see Clementine. He told her when the funeral was arranged for, and what the service would consist of. He also advised that she and her sisters should attend. Clementine simply held out an envelope in her hand, which as promised, contained the doctors fees.

After the doctor had gone, the whole house felt at ease, and the days of suppression had gone. It must have been a matter of weeks after the death of William, that the locals started to see seven sisters walking around the gardens, laughing and joking with one another, and dozens of cats, swirling around their legs.

CHAPTER 14

Many a night, the sisters would enter the large ballroom, which by now, was looking very shabby indeed. Violet would rush across to the old polyphone and place a penny in it. It would start to play, and the sisters would dance around the floor, from one sister to the next, re-enacting the balls that they themselves had missed because they were too young.

The mansion was always in darkness by ten o'clock, not a minute before, not a minute after. To the locals it seemed a little eerie. Once upon a day there were grand parties, now, there was nothing.

One day, Clementine was in the wash house humming a song to herself, one her mother used to sing years before. She was doing all the washing. Suddenly, Elizabeth ran in.

"Clementine, please, come quickly."

"What's wrong Elizabeth?" Clementine asked.

"It's Charlotte, it's Charlotte," she replied, tears rolling down her cheeks.

Clementine dropped the washing and ran out of the wash room, quickly followed by Elizabeth. She ran across the cobbled court yard and into the house, to find all her sisters gathered around Charlotte, who was laying on the floor. As she looked at Charlotte, she knew that she wasn't well, she knew that she must be put to bed immediately to rest. All the sisters carried Charlotte up the large staircase, towards the room they all used.

For many a night, they would all take turns sitting with Charlotte, wiping her face with a cold cloth as she constantly perspired.

One night, while all her other sisters slept, Clementine sat at the side of Charlotte's bed, it was her turn to nurse her sister. She could see that her condition was fast becoming worse. As she stared at the small, pitiful face, the youngest one of the family, she tried to think of a time that Charlotte showed any signs of being ill, but she couldn't think. Clementine was convinced that her baby sister had a severe cold and the moment that the fever broke, she would be well again.

Suddenly, a cord holding one of the smaller pictures that hung on the wall, snapped and the picture fell to the floor, probably, Clementine thought, because the cord was so old. The noise however woke Charlotte, who turned her head towards Clementine – the others just moaned, turned over and carried on sleeping.

"Sleep Charlotte." Clementine said gently, soothing her forehead with her fingers.

"I'm going where mother is Clementine." Charlotte said in a small shaky voice.

"No! *No!* Please, Charlotte, get some rest" Clementine pleaded. The minute that Clementine had spoken, Charlotte seemed to slip back into a restful sleep

Suddenly Clementine jumped. Her eyes opened. Her head was laying on the bed beside Charlotte's side, she was still holding one of her sisters hands. It was light, she must have fallen asleep. As she sat up looking at Charlotte, she noticed that her sister was breathing much heavier now. Her cheeks had sunk, making her nose look slightly bent and sharp.

Her other sisters had started to wake, first Violet, then Emily, and Victoria, followed by Elizabeth and Agnes. They all crawled out of bed and walked, still in their nightgowns, across the room to Charlotte's bed, and sat down.

"How is she?" Elizabeth asked.

"Resting" Clementine answered, "I think that this is the day we should call the doctor in."

Clementine asked her sisters to go downstairs and prepare the breakfast, and make a cup of tea, as it had been a long night. Four little sisters left the room, leaving Elizabeth sitting opposite Clementine on the bed.

"God help her." Elizabeth said as she started sobbing. "God help us!"

Clementine instantly had a cold feeling about her, a feeling that the family, for no reason, was breaking up. She took her eyes off Elizabeth, and looked again at Charlotte. She had a lump in her throat, which made it impossible for her to remain in the room any longer. She rose from the bed, making an excuse to Elizabeth that she had to supervise the rest of the sisters, and would return shortly. Then she left, heading for the kitchen and the others.

Whilst in the kitchen, Elizabeth came in.

"She's very restless Clementine, I think you had better check her again." Elizabeth stated.

Clementine left the kitchen, and wearily climbed the large staircase. She was *so* tired, she felt she was on the brink of fainting. As she opened the bedroom door, she couldn't believe her eyes. There, sat on the window stool, was Charlotte. She was holding the long velvet curtains, and rocking slightly. Clementine rushed across the room to her side.

"Come Charlotte," she said, "let me help you back to bed."

"Clementine, Clementine, I'm leaving this house. The gates are opening for me. I can see the track, without any bars in front of me. Come with me Clementine, come with me." Charlotte's hand slowly started to slide down the curtains, until she finally let go. She'd let go not only of the curtains, but of her life too. Charlotte slumped into Clementine's arms. At last, she was **FREE!**

Clementine held her tightly, not able to shout or ring for the rest of the sisters, she was in a state of shock. She felt numb, weak, bewildered. She lay her face down onto the top of Charlotte's head, kissing her and rocking her baby sister from side to side, humming the song her mother used to sing.

Her prolonged absence from the kitchen had been noticed by the sisters. As she was rocking Charlotte, she turned her head, and there standing in the doorway, were the rest of her sisters. Their hands clasped over their mouths, and forcing back tears, not one of them daring to make a sound, but each and every one of them knew that something had happened. Something that was going to affect the family from that day, and for the rest of their lives.

The remaining six sisters, sat with Charlotte until the following morning, then Clementine, once again was waiting, waiting for someone to pass those large iron gates. Someone she could ask to fetch the doctor for them.

Charlotte's death took its toll on the family. Charlotte was the baby of the family, the little bundle of joy that Clementine used to lay down and hold, whilst her and her sisters were huddled together, listening to their father. Charlotte's death was the straw that broke the camels back with the remaining Browning sisters. The doctor had been with the undertakers, and as usual, had cleaned up the family's dilemma, without any of the sisters having to venture through the gates, or anyone from the outside having to come in. But he knew what William had put these children through was beyond the call of duty. It shocked the remaining sisters so much, that they became even more withdrawn. Agnes was often the one that they had to find, sometimes she would be in the bedroom or sometimes the stables. Every-time that she was found, there was always a tear in her eyes. Agnes took Charlotte's death the hardest, being the one born just before her.

The weeks rolled on. As the days changed, so did the sisters. The days of laughter had gone, along with all the mock balls, and the sisters pretending that they were ladies. The only thing that stayed the same, was that the lights still went out at 10 pm.

CHAPTER 15

Clementine kept a close eye on Agnes as she was distancing herself more and more each day from the rest of the family. She'd often sit in the same room as the rest, but whilst they were talking, she would sit there staring into space.

One day, much the same as the last, they were all taking lunch, when suddenly, Emily noticed that Agnes wasn't in the room with them.

"Where's Agnes?" she asked.

But then she pre-occupied herself in conversation with Violet. Clementine, Elizabeth and Victoria suddenly looked at each other with stern concerned faces.

"I think we should look for her." Elizabeth said.

"Good idea," answered Clementine. "Let us split up and each search a part of the house. We all know she goes into the strangest places."

Emily and Violet stopped talking.

"Violet and I will search upstairs." Emily eagerly offered.

They all rose from their places and scurried out towards different parts of the house.

Twenty minutes later, they were all re-assembled in the hall – but still, no Agnes!

"Emily, Victoria, you two check the gardens, Violet, you check the stables, while Elizabeth and I will check the wash house and the other buildings."

They all took off to their stations to find Agnes. It had become a game again, the sort of thing that they used to play years ago when they were all young.

As the day progressed, and still with no sign of Agnes, they grew more and more concerned. Clementine walked down to the iron gates at the bottom of the garden, and gazed out onto the cart track that lead down towards Ryde town, wondering why after all these, she couldn't brave her way out into the wide world. She pressed her face against her hands that clutched the bars, and thought about Agnes. Her mind just seemed to float away, and she found that she was thinking about how her mother would stand a few feet behind her, while they were waiting for father to return home after a days business in Ryde. For those few split seconds, she felt warm and glowy, she felt that happy feeling that a child would have with such a close relationship with its parents. She smiled to herself.

In the distance she heard screams, which broke her out of her daydream. They were coming from behind her. They were distant but distinctive. Turning around sharply, she saw Elizabeth running towards her, shouting hysterically.

"Oh my god. Why! Why her!"

Clementine went cold. She knew that something drastic had befallen her family, and she had a feeling that she would never again talk or joke with Agnes, the second baby of her family. She stood there, rooted to the spot feeling numb, as Elizabeth fell to her knees, clutching her dress crying.

Clementine placed her hands on each side of her head, and looked up at the sky. Dear God, she thought, dear God what has happened! Violet, Emily and Victoria were soon standing at the side of Elizabeth, asking Clementine what the matter was, had Elizabeth hurt herself?

"She's dead isn't she Elizabeth. " Clementine stated, looking down at her trembling sister.

Elizabeth sobbed and sobbed. The others just stood there with eyes wide open, mouths not saying a word. Gradually, Elizabeth rose to her feet, and with eyes red from crying, looked Clementine straight in the eyes.

"Come." she said, then turned and walked towards the orchard.

Clementine and her sisters followed with apprehension. As they walked through the overgrown orchard, seeing a now composed Elizabeth in front of them, her long dress occasionally catching brambles, they knew that by the end of the day, not only Elizabeth, but the whole household, would be crying.

It seemed to take forever, clawing their way through the overgrown shrubs, and overhanging branches and brambles – which continuously plucked at their dressed, as if telling them not to continue. Finally, deep within the orchard, they came across a small clearing. Clementine was struck cold, she just stood there with the rest of her sisters behind her.

Elizabeth stood in front of them all, quiet, arms by her sides, motionless. No-body spoke a word, the rest of them chocking back the tears.

There Agnes swung, from side to side in the light breeze. She'd used an old piece of rope from the potting shed, and carefully chosen the tree to climb, just as she would have as a small child. The look on her face, was that of a person who had escaped one hell, only to end up in another.

Clementine fell to her knees. "Not Agnes," she sobbed. "Not Agnes. Help her, help her quickly, quickly!" she shouted in a shaky voice.

They all rushed towards Agnes, as if the tragedy had just happened. They gripped her around her legs and slightly lifted her until the rope went slack. Emily hastily scampered up the tree just like Agnes would have done hours earlier and untied the rope from the branch.

Softly laying their sister down on the fern that grew between the trees, the girls just knelt there, each and everyone of them, with their hands laid upon her. They had never come across any thing like this before, it was as if at any minute Agnes would spring to her feet and start to laugh – but she didn't.

Clementine and Elizabeth knew that this wasn't a game, and with their stern faces, the rest soon fell into suit. They all carried Agnes back through the trees and brambles, back towards the house, where they knew that the family doctor would take care of everything for them once again.

Once they had Agnes back at the house, Emily ran off to the kitchen to make a cup of tea for them all. As she walked back into the drawing room where they had laid Agnes on one of the chaise longues, Emily realised that she had made tea for seven of them -reality being lost in seconds! The tea was placed down onto one of the tables, the sisters were all slumped on the floor staring at the palish, blue face of Agnes. She hadn't spun to her feet laughing that she'd fooled them all, then run off into another room. This was quite different, she lay there motionless, with a purple mark around her neck. Clementine rose from her knees, then walked across towards the curtains, and slowly pulled them across.

Turning towards her sisters she softly said "Come, leave Agnes in peace until the doctor arrives."

They all rose from their knees, and walked out of the room towards the kitchen, thinking of how Clementine could make things right, make them back into a family again. By this time Clementine was exhausted, and wondering how she could console the emotions of her sisters.

She dragged a stand chair across the room, to the side of Agnes and sat down. She felt it was her place to spend Agnes's last night at home with her, she couldn't leave her on her own. None of them had ever had to spend a night alone.

She kept her eyes firmly fixed on her sister as she waited there, in anticipation, hoping that Agnes would open her eyes and ask her where had all the others had gone? Leaning over, she took Agnes's hand in hers and held it, wondering to herself, where had she gone wrong?

Clementine stayed with Agnes all night, knowing that when the doctor arrived in the morning with his two men, that that would be the last time she would ever see Agnes. At 3 o'clock, she wrote a note for the young lad that rode past their home, requesting that he contact the doctor, and ask him if he would call and see them urgently.

As she walked from the house down towards the large gates that early morning, she experienced all the early morning smells, the smell of the ferns and the flowers that had been purposely chosen by her parents for their party nights years ago. To Clementine, this was nothing new. She had been through her mothers death, her fathers death, then Charlotte's and now Agnes. What next, or, who next? Hers?

The doctor came the next morning, with the undertaker and his assistant, and as usual, cleared up the Browning sisters confusion. He really *was* a good man!

CHAPTER 16

Several months later, as Clementine was walking from the house towards the large gates at the bottom of the garden to place the order with the grocer for the forthcoming week, a young lad on his push bike was passing the entrance. He stopped suddenly to say good afternoon to Clementine. As they were talking, word came out that the village doctor – the Browning's doctor – had suddenly died in his sleep. On hearing this Clementine felt drained. She felt tingly all over, yet upset.

She rushed back to the house, her throat tightening, she kept thinking of who would take over next, and would they understand the sisters? Clementine was losing her focus on reality, she'd been a prisoner of that house for so long, that she as well as the others had been taking major things about the house too lightly.

She got to hear that the doctor who had taken over from the old family doctor was called Edwards, and that he would soon be visiting them. Would he understand she wondered, that none of them could possibly leave the grounds!

They all carried on life as usual. Up in the mornings, take breakfast, then dinner, then tea. Each and every morning the sisters carried out their duties, all except or one, Violet, who just did nothing. Clementine, Elizabeth, Emily and Victoria carried on their normal lives. Getting up, doing their duties, washing, tending the garden and whatever came within the scope of the day. Violet remained seated at the dining room table every day whilst they were working, just sat looking through the window and onto the lawns where the croquet matches were once played.

The doctor had visited all the patients whom he had inherited through the death of the old doctor – all barring one family – the Brownings. This was something to the doctor, this was a family of distinction, a family that people looked up to, albeit he'd heard they were very eccentric.

Clementine by now was starting to forget many things, and showed less and less concern over her remaining sisters. She had had a lifetime of being head of the family whilst her mother was too busy giving birth, and her father too drunk in his study to bother. Then the sudden death of her mother, leaving her to bring up her sisters. She was now too numb to reality to care, she was totally deprived of feeling!

The days passed, and in the evening the sisters would assemble in the dining room, oblivious to the fact the Violet was sat there. They would sit down with the few feeble scraps that had been prepared in the kitchens – cooking was a thing they they had never been taught. Young ladies from a certain standing in the community just didn't do things like that! A meal would be set down in front of Violet and the sisters would then start to talk about the days activities. Violet would always sit there not saying a word. The other girls would simply ignore this, and talk amongst themselves, not realising that Violet had not touched a scrap of food. After the meal, they would as usual, leave the table and take up residence in the drawing room, where they would pick up their needlework form the night before, and start to add stitch after stitch, and watch as the picture on their mind unfolded onto the material.

The following morning they would assemble in the dining room for what small breakfast they could prepare for themselves. They'd all sit down in their usual places chatting away merrily amongst themselves. Violet would be sat in her place, not saying a word. The other sisters were all used to this by now, so they simply ignored it.

Clementine would occasionally say "toast Violet?" Then she would get up from her chair, and take a slice down the long table, and place it in front of her. She would immediately return to her seat after giving Violet the toast, and sit down.

Two weeks had passed, then one early morning, there was a knock at the front door. Emily rushed out of the kitchen and along the huge hall towards the front door. As she opened it, there stood the doctor. He had saved his visit to them to the last. On announcing himself to Emily, she asked him in. He immediately took out his handkerchief, and held it towards his nose. The smell was awful! It was a smell that he knew all to well, it was the smell of death.

It wasn't the smell of a dead dog or cat, or even several rats. This was the unmistakable smell of rotting human flesh. Still holding his handkerchief to his nose, he told Emily that he was their new family doctor, and being an inquisitive man, he had to find out where that stench was coming from, and what had happened to cause it. Emily, full of smiles and the joys of spring, told him to follow her to where the rest of the sisters were, the dining room. The doctor feeling very uneasy followed.

As he walked into the dining room behind Emily, the smell was so intense, that it made him feel rather sick.

"Good morning" Clementine said, standing from her chair followed by the rest of her sisters.

"Good morning Miss Browning" the doctor replied, still holding his handkerchief tight to his nose. "I have called to let you know that I am your doctor from now on, and I hope that I can be of service to you, the same as your old doctor before me."

"Thank you Doctor Edwards" Clementine said. "Would you please take a seat and have some breakfast with us?"

"I'll take a seat, but no breakfast for me thank you, I have already eaten."

The minute Clementine mentioned breakfast, his stomach had begun to heave. After sitting at the side of Clementine he glanced across the table to the other sisters faces. They were all smiling, just as they had done for the last several years. As his eyes settled on Violet, the grip of horror grasped him. God have mercy, he thought, this person is dead, and they don't even care. He rose from his seat. "Don't you ladies realise she's dead!" he shouted. All the sisters just stared at him, as if her was beginning to have a fit.

"Are you all right?" Clementine enquired in a sincere voice.

"God woman!" he screamed. "She's **dead**"

One by one, starting with Clementine, the sisters gently swung their heads towards Violet. Clementine rose from her chair and gracefully walked down, past her sisters who were still sitting at the long table, to the side of Violet. She put her hand on Violet's shoulder, then knelt down by her side. She gazed into her semi-decomposed face for several minutes, then looked up and back to the doctor.

"I believe she is." she said. "Would you help us with her arrangements please doctor?"

Dr. Edwards jumped from his chair. All the sisters still gazing over to Violet. The doctor tried to make it to the dining room door, but fell to his knees by the side of one of the old stand chairs and vomited.

"Don't worry doctor," Clementine said, "we'll take care of that."

77

As the doctor left the house, he paused on the patio of the front door which led down the large stone steps and into the garden. The stench of Violet clung to his tongue. It repeatedly made him feel sick.

Snapping herself out of stupefaction, Clementine requested that all the doors and windows must be opened, right the way through the house. All the other sisters ran to their own stations, doing what Clementine had asked. None of them had noticed the vile smell due to their mental state by this time, and so living with it day by day had become accustomed to it.

Twenty minutes later and the doctor was back with a selected few men, and a police officer to to remove the body of Violet, the third Browning sister to escape, be it to a better place or not, none of the sisters knew.

CHAPTER 17

Over the following months, it was discovered that Violet had died through natural causes. It caused great concern with the authorities and the locals alike, as to why the Browning sisters had lived with a corpse for all that length of time, it was put down to the eccentric ways of the sisters, and like most nine day wonders, it was all soon forgotten.

Late one night, weeks after Violet had died, the landing of the house was lit with the flashes of lightning from a violent storm. Clementine was woken to the sound of screaming. She quickly rose from her bed and put her robe on. The door to the room they shared was slightly ajar. She could see parts of the landing outside of the room. She could see the carpet that ran down the centre of the landing, and the large white marble bust of a past relative. She groped for the oil lamp at the side of the mantle over the fireplace. Turning the wick up giving her more light, she walked across to the bedroom door, and out onto the landing. As she turned to her left, which had the top of the stairs in sight, she could see Victoria standing there holding the handrails. She hurried along the landing until she was stood directly behind Victoria, who swung round to face Clementine. Her eyes were wide with an insane glare about them. This took Clementine back. She was frightened for the first time in her life. With a flash of lightning on Victoria's face she saw her father as he was in his days when he was avoiding Amelia. It all came back to Clementine in those few seconds. Clementine turned her head to compose herself, then just as quick, turned her head back to face Victoria, who looked completely different. She looked like a frightened young child who had just woken steps away from her bed.

"What is it Victoria?" Clementine asked. "Are you all right?"

Victoria looked softly into Clementine's eyes, with tears rolling down her face.

"Violet." Victoria said. "Violet."

"What about Violet?" Clementine asked carefully.

"She wants me to go and play with her in the gardens."

"No" Clementine said. "You are dreaming dear. Come with me back to your bed and rest."

Clementine slowly placed her hand on Victoria's, and gently prised her sisters fingers from the banister rail.

"Come" she said. "It'll be fine in the morning, you'll see."

They both walked back towards their room each one of them to their bed.

Victoria quietly said "It's time Clementine, it's time"

Clementine told her to close her eyes and dream of things that had passed. Nice things. Then suddenly, there was no more sound coming form Victoria's bed. Clementine lay there, she was breathing faster and was wide awake. She thought of the days when all of her sisters were together. Then suddenly, Emily was shaking her, it was morning.

She sat up in bed and scanned the room, all the beds were empty. She could remember the night before, but still she had doubts as to if it had actually happened or was it just a dream. Emily swiftly left the room, and shortly after, Clementine was beside her remaining sisters in the dining room taking breakfast.

As she ate her breakfast, she kept glancing over to Victoria, still with doubts in her mind, but Victoria was there smiling with her other sisters, as if last night had never happened. It gave Clementine a very uneasy feeling, a feeling that she now had to watch her younger sister, just to prove that her premonition could be wrong. Clementine had and uneasy feeling that Victoria would be short lived. The very look on Victoria's face gave off that aura of poor health. She had that waxy look about her face, and her features were growing sharper.

After they had eaten, they all took their dishes to the kitchen and washed them. That was a long standing arrangement, the rule had been made when they were small. A rule that Clementine had made whilst in the years of her mother's hardships. Clementine sat at the dining room table just looking at the chairs which lay there at the table. There were now four chairs, and she often wondered how long it would be before there was three. Her eyes once again filled with tears. She got up, and carried her dish to the kitchen, she could hear the rest of her sisters giggling and laughing somewhere on the landing upstairs.

By now the house was very drab looking and the grounds were well overgrown. The paintwork inside the house was flaking, and all the curtains, and lace material smelt of musk, looked dirty and were in need of a wash. Time marched on, and Clementine's worries about Victoria soon left her mind as she continued with her daily chores.

The day that brought Clementine's worries back, was the day that Victoria entered the bedroom one afternoon complaining of a very sore throat. Clementine tentatively placed her hand on Victoria's face and moved her head back until she could see what the problem was with her throat. As she looked down her sister's throat, she could see large yellow headed ulcers, which she knew was a normal sign of infection. She told her sister to go and wash her mouth out with salt water. This went on and on for weeks, resulting in Victoria not being able to take anything in solid form. Victoria soon started to loose weight. Pound after pound fell of her already slight body, showing mostly about her face. She started to take to her bed during the day, complaining that she felt sick and had a headache. Clementine could see that through her ongoing frailty, Victoria was detaching herself more and more from the family. Was this natures way of taking the pain away from the family if anything should happen to her? Clementine was by now, so confused, and with no help or advice didn't know what to think.

One very early morning, there she was standing at the large iron gates, one again, waiting for the early morning boy on his cycle to ride by. Once she'd passed the message on to him to give to Doctor Edwards, she knew that it would only be hours before he was there tending to Victoria.

After all those weeks since the storm, Victoria would just sit in front of the bedroom window rambling to herself.

As Clementine expected, the doctor was there within hours of receiving the note and she was sitting in one of the drawing rooms when he walked in after examining Victoria.

"Your sister is very ill." he said.

"I know" replied Clementine. "Is she dying doctor? Is she dying?"

The doctor paused for a while as now he new what the family had been through. "Yes Miss Browning. I'm afraid she is." was his reply, as he dropped his head.

"Don't be embarrassed doctor, at least you are telling me the truth."

"In all my years of practice Miss Browning, I have never held back the truth from anyone in this position, and I do not intend starting now."

Clementine although underweight, knowing what his answer would be, felt a sharp jab in her stomach, followed by a cold tingling feeling. "What is wrong with her and how long has she got doctor?"

"Who knows Miss Browning, months, weeks, days. I have had several patients like this before, they loose weight rapidly, then just fade away. I wish I knew what it was. If only I could stop it."

Clementine walked across to the drawing room door and opened it. "Thank you for you frankness.", she said.

When the doctor had left, she walked back over to the window and watched him walk away from the house, down the pathway towards the large iron gates. As she watched him, she knew deep down in her stomach, that was by no means the last time that she would watch him walk up and down that path. She now realised that those days of happy, giggling sisters, when death was the furthest thought in their head had ended. Her childish dreams, that everyone holds, of them all being together forever, had struck reality.

Over the next few months, the doctor frequently visited the house, until it was finally the time for Victoria to give up. She died peacefully in her bed early one morning, a few days short of what the the doctor had predicted. Cause of death – heart failure.

There were no exceptions to the rule, the remaining sisters dare not cross over that barrier from their pathway, through the gates and onto the track that led towards Ryde. Doctor Edwards took care of everything for the family. Now there were only three of them left. Clementine, Elizabeth and Emily.

This could have been a huge family, filled with daughters, sons-in-law and grandchildren, but no. This was the result of William, their father, who had made choices for his children. How could one man cause so much pain and suffering to his own daughters.

CHAPTER 18

For months and months after the death of Victoria, the three remaining sisters would sit either by the fire if it was cold at nights, or on the patio outside the front door if it was warm, all saying nothing, just reminiscing of days past.

The three of them would rise in the morning and take breakfast. Their next task, would be feeding all the cats they had such a soft spot for, because the cat the they had first taken in had had kittens, and these in turn had had kittens. There were now around one hundred of them, and feeding took up most of the morning, and sometimes, well into the afternoon.

The three of them lived a reasonably happy life for a time after the death of Victoria. Then Emily became ailing and withdrawn. Suddenly there were two. The same had happened to Emily, she left the house early one morning with the help of the doctor. She had died peacefully in her sleep. Again, natural causes were diagnosed. This was too much for Clementine, who spent most of her days and nights crying over the loss of sisters. That often left Elizabeth, who caught her crying and it would often take several hours to console her, and to look after the daily chores. The two sisters were a definite picture of girls, who had been deprived of a life.

Over the ensuing years, Clementine became very frail, and frequently had memory lapses, which put a great deal of strain on Elizabeth. The final blow came when that little girl, playing with the grass, plucking daisy heads, chuckling happy in the sunshine. The little girl, who was once, many, many years ago, the apple of her daddy's eye. The little girl, who once of a day, had so much to live for, so much to be happy about, but through fates cruel blows, lived a life of imprisonment. Finally, through ill health, and memory failing, she gave up her fight, and went on that journey, through those large iron gates for the first, and last time on her own, to join her sisters that she loved so much, and the mother, who was so cruelly taken from her all those years ago.

Once again, the doctor arranged everything, and Elizabeth watched as her older sister left to be entombed again, but this time in death.

That left poor Elizabeth, all alone in that big old grey house. Her only comfort and companionship, her memories and the feeding of the hundred cats.

Clementine had given up her fight one afternoon after taking tea with Elizabeth. She rose from her chair in the drawing room, telling Elizabeth that she felt tired, and was going to lie down. Half way up the stairs, she slumped to her knees, head pressed against the stairs, her hand still clutching the handrail. She gave out a shriek, and gasped for breath.

Elizabeth, who had been startled by the noise, ran to her sister's side. "What is wrong Clementine?" she'd asked.

Clementine just stared at the carpet in front of her. Slowly releasing the handrail, and sliding her hand down the spindles, she whispered, "I'm sorry, I'm so sorry. Who is going to look after you now Elizabeth?"

"You are Clementine, you are."

Clementine gave her last gasp of breath and remained motionless. She had died.

CHAPTER 19

Elizabeth was left standing in the hall, just staring at the door. Where had they all gone? Where were they all? She could hear the old grandfather clock ticking away from the landing upstairs. The clock had been kept religiously wound by Clementine since their father had died. The tick seemed to be magnified at the moment, but nothing else. The house was dismal, dark and eerily quiet.

She turned, then slowly walked back into the drawing room. She picked up Clementine's embroidery, and put it into a draw with the rest of the sisters embroidery, just as if it was an every day occurrence. She went over to her embroidery, the one that she'd dropped when Clementine had collapsed. She sat in one of the winged chairs, and started sewing. It was like she had lost all sense of reality. It was like she was waiting for her sisters to burst in the room, all laughing and giggling, then sit down and pick up their needlework.

By now, Elizabeth too was failing fast, and it was only by the keen, careful, watching eye of her neighbours, who hadn't seen her wondering the grounds, that they asked the local doctor to visit.

The doctor, in-between patients, rested back in his swivel chair. He swung to the side, and gazed out of the widow. He suddenly realised that he hadn't seen the last remaining daughter of William and Amelia Browning for years. He decided that he would visit her after his surgery, he swung his chair around again, and put his finger on his bell. He remembered the day he'd found Violet, and could still smell the stench of her rotting body. To think that she'd been sat there for two weeks. That smell would stay with him for the rest of his life.

Three o'clock soon came – it was the end of his surgery. He felt ill himself. He stood up from his chair, not really wanting to visit the Browning house, and thinking of all the excuses he could, to get out of his duties. He knew that if he did not go, then he would be looked down upon by all the local community with her being old and frail and on her own. Attending was a must!

Elizabeth was plodding along doing her daily duties, unaware that the doctor was going to visit, until the banging on the front door started.

As the doctor stood waiting for the door to open, he could feel his stomach turning. It was like eating a piece of fish that made you feel very ill, then months later, lifting another piece on your fork – the smell turning your stomach. As he stood there, he took two deep breaths. He was preparing himself for what might hit him the moment the door opened.

Elizabeth finally opened the door after her long trek from her bedroom, where she was having her afternoon nap. As the door opened, there she stood with an over-powering smell of flowery perfume. During the day, she'd filled the house from top to bottom with flowers.

"Come, come in Doctor Edwards." she beckoned him in.

The doctor crossed over into her world. The world of fine things, paintings, busts and furniture, which all held the smell of must and dampness of yesterday's world.

"I've called to see how you are handling things these days, and to see how your health is" the doctor stated.

"Fine doctor. Let us go in to the dining room."

Walking into the dining room, he imagined the smell from years before, and his stomach turned once again. He quickly found the nearest chair and sat down. This is silly he thought. There's no smell, it's all in my head. They talked for several hours, then he left, but this time, not realising that in the very near future, he would become a very rich man. They talked about him calling in every night after his surgery, so that he could make sure she was all right.

One evening, as the doctor called on Elizabeth, he noticed that the front door was wide open. It had been a very hot day, in fact it had been very hot for several weeks, and the Isle of Wight Council, and many more councils throughout Britain had called a drought emergency. He walked up the large stone steps to the front of the house, and tapped his cane on the open front door, hoping that he would hear her frail voice calling him in. He stood there for several minutes without any response, then suddenly he remembered how Clementine had died walking up the stairs, he went cold. Dropping his cane, he started to run into the old house and towards the staircase, he ran up the stairs and into the room that Elizabeth used.

"Doctor" he heard from behind him. Swivelling round he saw Elizabeth in the door way.

"Thank God, your all right" was all he could gasp.

"Yes. No cause for concern Doctor Edwards." Elizabeth replied.

"I thought............"

"I know, you thought I'd gone with my sisters. No harm done Doctor Edwards." she said. "Please, come with me. I've got something on my mind, and I wish to have your advice."

She walked past him, clutching her little straw basket filled with flowers. She took him through into the drawing room, then placed the basket of flowers down on a very highly polished French Loo table.

"Please be seated " she requested. "There's a terrible drought all over the country – so one of my neighbours tells me."

The doctor was instantly taken aback. It was as if Elizabeth had been into the town of Ryde to visit a friend, but he knew this wasn't so. Where had she received this information from, he wondered.

"How have you heard that?" he asked puzzled.

She smiled gently, "from a local farmer" she replied. "I was at the large gates this morning, leaving my order for the grocer, when the farmer passed, he told me then. Any way, the reason that we must talk is, I have decided that nobody here on the Isle of Wight will *ever* be subjected to a no water situation, not now or in the future."

The doctor just sat there, hour after hour listening to Elizabeth and her views that the councils were not doing enough for the people of this Country. He was quite surprised that a lady of her years and standing had so many views, after literally being a prisoner for all these years.

"I must leave now," he said standing up.

"Doctor," Elizabeth said. "Could I ask you a small favour?"

"Yes." he relied.

"Here's twenty pounds. Could you, I trust that you will be calling tomorrow night?"

"Yes."

"Could you bring some ice-cream, a bottle of Champagne, and a few shillings for my gas meter?" she asked.

"Certainly" he answered. "For just as long as you wish."

After he'd left the house, Elizabeth walked across to the drawers that held all the needlework that her sisters had been doing, she held them for a few minutes, then singling out the last one to be placed in the drawer – Clementine's – tears started to roll down her cheeks. It was as if, just holding that piece of material, she was holding onto her memories and childhood.

The following night, the doctor true to his word arrived at the Browning house with her requested items. She told the doctor that she wished that a well be dug for the people of the Isle of Wight, and the place that it was to be dug, was of the doctor's choosing. She would, of course, provide the finance.

That night, as the doctor left the Browning estate, he racked his brains for the spot that not only she would be pleased with, but the most practical place, with underground streams. After many talks with local people and council members, he decided that the the well would be dug at St. Lawrence, near Ventnor.

The night after he returned to Elizabeth, and told her of the place near Ventnor that he'd chosen, but that she should think very slowly about it until she was very sure. Elizabeth did, for almost thirty seconds.

"Doctor Edwards, go ahead," was all that she said.

CHAPTER 20

Over the following months, Doctor Edwards organised everything and achieved what Elizabeth had requested. The moment that the well had been dug, it was in all the local newspapers. It had its official opening, and was in operation, all without Elizabeth ever being there. The Council named the road leading up to the well – Seven Sisters Road.

The day finally came when this world was no longer in stride with Elizabeth's world. She could not fit in with all the modern things that were going on around her, motor cars, radio, even television. This was a world that was so different from hers – her needlework, her cats and bed by 9.30pm after a day in the gardens – that was Elizabeth's world.

After a normal day, Elizabeth retired to bed, then peacefully slipped back through her thoughts, then eventually, through those large iron gates, just like her sisters had done years before – not in body, but in spirit and soul. At last she too was *free!* Free from all the adjusting to modern life. Free only a few hours before her trusted friend, Doctor Edwards could say goodbye. There she lay in the bed that frail, long haired grey old lady – Elizabeth. At the side of her bed, lay a book which she had been reading, a book of nobility called Burke's Peerage. The moment that she drew her last breath, the house also died around her.

The doctor called the morning after, and being such a trusted friend, let himself in with the key he'd been given. He searched all the rooms, and eventually found Elizabeth in her bed. He didn't feel sad, but relief to finally know that after all these years of solitude, she was now reunited with her sisters, all seven of them playing somewhere in God's large garden. He smiled at the thought.

As usual Doctor Edwards arranged everything for Elizabeth, just as he had done for her sisters. Then, just like her sisters, her body followed the path down towards those large iron garden gates, to be opened for the last time, to let her fly free.

Elizabeth ventured out into that big wide world for a short time, only to be imprisoned once again, in a cemetery, not more than half a mile away.

After the formalities of Elizabeth's funeral, the doctor returned back to the house of this once fine family. Elizabeth, over the last few years of her life, had told him of her intentions at the time of her death. As he walked back into the house, hours after her burial, he just stood in the hall. It was cold with a deathly silence. He could hear the distant echoes of the past. The laughter, the music and the cries of anguish. It was as if all the foundations had stored the vibrations from the past. He quickly turned and made haste through the front door. For the first time in his life, he was frightened. As he reached the patio outside the front door, he felt sick.

After that day, he ordered that the whole place be boarded up until the time of the reading of the will.

All that Elizabeth had promised the doctor came true. He inherited all her money, all the money that had been passed down from the death of her sisters which totalled up to just over one million pounds. The house, and all its contents was left in trust to the sisters after their fathers death, but who was going to claim the estate. Not the sisters, as William always wanted a son and heir, someone to carry on the family name. The house was boarded up, and the doctor received his money. The heir was eventually traced by the aide of solicitors to France. To everyone's surprise, he didn't want to know a penny of the estate. He was happily living a simple life in a Monastery. Nobody cared anyway. The house just lay boarded up with all the furniture in it belonging to no-one.

Time went on, and eventually Doctor Edwards died leaving his wife and children very well off indeed.

During the next two years following the death of the doctor, the house caught fire twice. Some say it was the act of local thieves who deliberately fired the place to cover their tracks. It obviously fooled the police, as there were no prosecutions. Then there were the views of other people who knew, or had been told the tale of these sad sisters, who firmly believed that the burning was an end, by the sisters spirits, to stop any publicity of the Browning name. After the second fire at the house the council inspected the premises, and decided the remains of the once grand mansion should be demolished. They found little evidence of furniture or antiques, as they had all been stolen over the years. They ordered that after the demolition of the house, all the remaining furniture be sold at auction, and the proceeds given to the surviving relatives of the late Doctor Edwards.

While they were demolishing the house, several workmen reported seeing a tall, grey haired old lady dressed in long clothes walking about the grounds. Many a sighting was reported around the area which was the study, and the room that was used by Amelia. The description that was given by these workmen was of Clementine. It seemed that Clementine was there to the end, looking after all the places that held her memories. After the first sighting was reported, it made it very hard for the demolition company to carry out their work, as all the men they employed quit their jobs after a few days. It was only when a local doctor from another town who heard the story volunteered to be there on the day of the demolition, the work carried on.

Suddenly there was total quietness. I looked around. The birds had stopped making their twittering sound, it was deathly quiet. I was looking all around, trying to see why the birds had stopped making a noise. Then a cold, tingling feeling flowed through me. Where the hell was the old man I'd just been talking too? The bench beside me was empty, and suddenly I was standing fifteen feet in front of it, looking back upon it. Had he slipped away minutes before my imagination had taken over? I walked from the clearing, from that bench, from the remains of the house with its over grown gardens, I was very confused.

Several days later, curiosity got the better of me, and I had to return to the place where I'd heard this very unusual story. As I walked through the old iron gates once more, I just could not find the clearing with the old bench that I'd sat on for several hours only a few days earlier. I felt easy, yet frightened, maybe because they'd persuaded me to write their story, to tell the truth. It must have been like being a prisoner in a cracker – making factory, the only way of making people listen, is to put the message in a cracker.

When you think about it, what a waste of a family, their whole life, their whole world, just a few acres of garden and several rooms. It's a wonder that they kept their sanity for as long as they did.

~~~~~

As I have already said, there is a three bedroomed bungalow standing on the grounds of the old Carter mansion. For myself, and Hilary, walking around the ruins, we could feel very strongly, a sense that the grounds still held the vibrations form those magnificent balls that used to be held there night after night, in the Seven Sisters living tomb!

The story that I have told about those seven sisters,
had to be written.
Whether it be a documentary, or a novel,
it doesn't matter. It's now told.

NOW, THE CAN REST!